CHA

BOUND BY KNIGHTHOOD

BOUND BY KNIGHTHOOD

STARRY KINGDOMS OF THE FAE BOOK EIGHT

NICKI CHAPELWAY

DRAGONFLIGHT PRESS

CONTENTS

To everyone who ever dreamed of becoming a knight.

CHAPTER ONE

B yron should be a cursed word. Instead, it's a boy's name. Not just any boy though, the sweetheart of the whole village. Byron Coalbiter, grandson of a blacksmith, and with his unfortunately easy looks and powerful magic, he's basically had success handed to him on a silver platter.

But that isn't enough for him. No, he can't just lead a prosperous life, he has to steal *my* success and run off with my dreams and coerce away my future. I wrinkle my nose at the very thought. I've worked my tailbone off to get admitted into this academy. As a fae born of low-magic, I have no influence of my own, to my fellow fae. To them, I'm no better than the humans whose blood likely flows in my veins, weakening my magic and inherited from some distant ancestor. But this academy is my chance to change all that.

If I can get a high fae to notice me and claim me as their knight, then I can get them to grant me a portion of their magic. I just need a portion. That combined with my own magic, and I'll finally be exceptional enough to no longer be a disgrace.

"What do you mean that he is attending the Academy of the Gilded Knights?" I spit out at last, breaking the heavy silence.

Marvin quirks his eyebrow, his apple halfway to his mouth. He reaches up to wipe juice off his round, freckled cheeks. "Did you think they *wouldn't* admit him, Willow?"

"I *thought* he would realize that he had enough and take his lucky lot in life and run off with some fae maiden who doesn't care about mixed blood descendants. Not that he would try to steal a knighthood right out from underneath me."

The apple crunches as Marvin takes another bite, he stares at the colors streaking the sky over the field his father owns. As the son of the wealthiest farmer in town, Marvin could likely have been the most popular boy in town. Instead, *Byron Coalbiter* stole all the fame and lovestruck girls from him. Luckily for him though, I've always hated Byron so Marvin has at least one ally. Now if only he would see it that way, but unfortunately Marvin stubbornly refuses to see Byron as competition. He even goes so far as to claim that the twice-blessed son of a bartering upstart is "all right by his book" and "that he doesn't see why I hate him so."

What I can't understand is why no one else hates him. Can't they see that twinkle of superiority in his eyes? That dratted glint, oh how the very sight of it makes my blood boil. And then there's his annoying habit of laughing between almost every sentence, like he finds your excuse for an existence so amusing he can't even stop laughing at it long enough to have a proper conversation.

There's also the fact that everything is so effortless for him. He's barely had to raise his little finger and already he has everything a soul could want. Love, adoration, and loyalty from the whole village. A pretty face—although he'll never hear the admission from me. Powerful magic that sets him above other humans and low-fae. And if that all failed, he even has a trade to fall back on: smithing.

He doesn't know what it is like to see others walk away with the very thing he wanted, nor would he ever understand what it is like to be laughed at by him.

I've tried to explain this all to Marvin. His only response is to say that I'm *jealous* of Byron. I nearly snort just remembering that. The very idea rings of madness. I wouldn't trade anything for what Byron has because little as I have at least, I've worked hard for it.

"So, do you think I'm trying to steal your knighthood because I'm also going?" he asks at last, startling me from my brooding.

I blink and turn to him, trying to make out my friend's features in the dim lighting of the sun disappearing behind the horizon. "What?"

Marvin tosses away the rest of his apple so the birds can have a chance at having a hearty meal. "You're so mad about this because you think Byron is going to steal your knighthood, but I'm going to the academy as well." He shrugs. "Hundreds of people from across the realm are going. Why don't you feel threatened by us?"

I bite my tongue to keep from telling Marvin that I could never be threatened by him. He might take it the wrong way. Instead, I push to my feet, brushing dead grass off the back of my pants and hold a hand out to him. He squints at it, clearly expecting an answer.

"You're only going because your father has delusions of grandeur," I say at last, trying to figure out the best way to phrase it without insulting him. We're going to be setting out for the Academy tomorrow, and it will be a long journey if he spends it all mad at me. "You don't even particularly want to go, do you?"

He shrugs, finally accepting my hand. I hoist him to his feet, before turning and starting back toward the large dark outline that's Marvin's house. "Your father wants you to get a knightship so that you might get some magic. Your family already has money and land, that's the only thing you're missing."

That's the only thing most humans are missing. Fae too though, aren't I proof of that? Not everyone is born with magic, and those that are... well it isn't always something worth writing home about. But I suppose it's the nature of people to want to extend beyond their lots.

Marvin wraps his arms around himself, his head ducked low as he shuffles after me. "Admit it, you're not worried about me because we all know the only reason I'm attending the Academy is because my father greased some palms. Once classes start it's going to show how unprepared I am. I didn't work hard to get there, not like you and Byron."

I scoff. "Byron did not work hard."

Marvin turns, narrowing his eyes at me.

"And you'll do just fine in your studies," I hurriedly add, holding up my hands to placate him. "You know I'll help you where I can."

"I can't just ride on your shoulders the whole way through."

"Why not? I have broad shoulders." Not as broad as Byron's though... bulls, why is that boy always better at everything?

Marvin shakes his head. "I have *some* self-respect, Willow."

"I know. I know. And you'll do fine. I'm not trying to make you feel bad by worrying about Byron, I'm sure we'll be very healthy competition to each other. It's just..." I trail off with a sigh, reaching up to pinch the bridge of my nose where a headache started ever since Marvin mentioned that Byron would also be going to the academy this year. "I'm going to be working to catch the eye of Lord Menavillion, and we all know that Byron has a family history with him. After all, it's Menavillion's magic that Byron wields! He practically has one foot already on the knighting platform."

"So then go for a different fae lord?"

"Menavillion is more than just some fae lord. He is a *high* fae. His magic is more powerful than what most people can even dream of," I say, rolling my eyes. "He is looking for a single student to fill an open position as his knight. I *will* be that student."

"If you say so," Marvin replies, his voice dry. "Sounds like you have your work cut out for you." He stifles a yawn. "But let's not talk about that anymore. Tomorrow will bring its own troubles, let's just enjoy our last night before we have to leave home."

CHAPTER TWO

W ell, Marvin was right. The next day did bring its own troubles. They walked up on a pair of black boots that were so shiny I could see my reflection in them half a league away.

My eyes widen, and I force them to drag up the person who belongs to the boots, although I know who it is even before I catch sight of his face. Only one person would walk through the muddy streets of our village in boots that polished.

Byron Coalbiter.

I stiffen, whipping my head to Marvin only to see him raise his hand in a wave, a pleasant smile on his face. "What are you doing?" I hiss out of the corner of my mouth.

"Being friendly, you should try it sometime."

"What is *he* doing here—" I cut myself off when I turn back to see that Byron has managed to close the distance between us and is now standing a short distance away. Well, within earshot. I cross my arms, narrowing my eyes. "What are you doing here?"

He has the audacity to chuckle. "Hello to you too, Willow."

I sniff, still waiting for an answer to my question. Byron blinks once, his smile sliding just a little bit before he turns to Marvin. "Nice weather for traveling." He tilts his head back, squinting at the sky. "Couldn't have picked a better day myself."

"Oh, no," I mumble, drawing both the boy's attention to me. "No, no, no. Do *not* tell me that he is joining us."

"And what would you rather I tell you instead?" Byron asks, amusement lacing his tone. His eyes have that dratted twinkle in them, the one that speaks of superiority.

"That you've opted to jump into a vipanther pit."

"Sounds painful," he replies, unfazed.

"Willow!" Marvin gasps, throwing me a bulging eye glance.

Byron's lip twitches upward slightly as he hikes an eyebrow. "Someone woke up on the wrong side of the haystack today."

I bristle at his implication that I don't have a proper bed. As the village orphan, I've borrowed from the kindness of everyone around me, staying in barns or on dirt floors next to the hearth. Doing chores and odd jobs in exchange for a place to sleep and whatever food that they can spare to give me.

In a village as poor as Woodsbury Grove, it's likely that I put a lot of good folks out of their ways to provide for me, but it isn't as if I asked to be born penniless and powerless, abandoned by whoever my parents were.

"I'll have you know that I have a bed," I snarl out. "Well, technically it's Marvin's bed but..." I trail off as my thoughts begin to catch up to my tongue, and I notice Marvin grow as red as his hair, making the light streaking the dawn ridden sky envious of the hues he has managed to achieve. Byron's smile slides off his face before it returns with more force. I hold up my hands. "Not like that though—he—I—we're just friends."

Marvin slaps his face into his hand. "Please stop talking," he whispers. "I think you're only making this worse."

"I disagree. It just keeps getting better and better." Byron is full-on grinning now, revealing all his straight white teeth. He bounces a little on the toes of those ridiculously shiny black boots. He flips his bound hair over his shoulder. I've heard some ladies in town compare the color of his hair to the bark of a weeping willow tree. Personally, I think it more resembles dirt, but no one other than me is comparing it to that.

My hair is brown as well, and decidedly *not* dirt colored due to the reddish hues in it, and I'm *named* Willow, but I don't hear anyone describing my hair as being the same color as, well, anything. No one is talking about my hair actually. Which is probably best seeing how little I washed it when I was younger. Now between Marvin and his father's hospitality, and the river that flows a few leagues from town I'm able to keep it clean, but when I was younger, I was too scared to stray very far from the village.

I bet no one has ever seen Byron with dirty hair.

One of the most unfortunate things about Byron, is his looks. I might just hate him a little less if he were ugly. At least then it wouldn't seem as if he didn't have every star in the sky align at his birth to create a perfect human with a perfect little life.

Byron glances at the bags near my feet, they're full of the few possessions I've managed to collect over the years. He looks back up at us then squints at the sky. "You ready to go?"

"I am....?" I begin slowly, my eyes flicking from my bags then to him, then to the strap of the satchel he adjusts where it is slung over his shoulder. Apart from those ridiculous boots, now that I think of it, he is dressed for travel in a worn coat and a sword attached to his side. Not that someone with his magical prowess really needs a sword, but I suppose since we are hoping to become knights, we might as well grow used to wielding swords.

"You sound so sure," he says, rolling his eyes. "Either you're ready or you need more time but stop standing there gawking at me. We're wasting sunlight."

"*We*?" I demand, I turn to Marvin who is looking everywhere but at me. "There is no *we*. There is just me and Marvin."

"Uh... Byron is coming with us," Marvin whispers, finally raising his gaze to meet mine.

"What?" I demand, already shaking my head. I suppose I had already suspected it, but it's truly cruel when all hope of that being untrue is snatched away. "No, no he isn't."

"We were already heading in the same direction. It's best that we stick together." His eyes dart from me to Byron, his cheeks coloring slightly.

"You know I'd protect you, Marvin," I hiss. "We don't need him."

"But then who would protect me?" Byron asks, his mouth turning up into a lopsided grin.

I roll my eyes. As if the magical prodigy of Woodsburry Grove needs protection.

"Seriously, though, if we are to make it to the academy before dark we should get going now."

"We should!" Marvin pipes up, he shoots me a desperate look as if pleading with me to stop arguing. I groan, bending over and grabbing my bags. I loop them over my arm. I already look bad enough saying Byron can't come, if I keep insisting it then I'm just going to make myself appear worse.

And I'm already low enough in Byron's eyes, best not to give him any more ammunition to throw at me. Besides, I'll be seeing plenty of him at the academy anyways, so it isn't as if I'll be getting away from him anytime soon

No, it seems I'm stuck with Byron Coalbiter a bit longer. But hopefully when I manage to find a way to keep Byron from stealing my dreams and achieve my knighthood, I'll be able to move far away from him. Him and his smug little smirk.

Now that will be the day.

CHAPTER THREE

I already knew that this was going to be a long trip without the addition of Byron. Marvin wasn't made for traveling... or anything strenuous easily. His fair skin blisters in the sun, and he has difficulty breathing sometimes, especially when he has been moving too much.

Not exactly the best qualities to find in a farmer's son, but fortunately for him his father is wealthy enough to hire men, so he doesn't have to work in the fields. No, his father has risen so far above his station, accumulated so much land and so much wealth that now he has high aspirations for his son.

Knighthood.

Not just any knighthood though, a Gilded Knighthood. There are other factions an aspiring knight could join such as the Hallowed Knights or the Knight of the Order or

Brotherhood, but none come with quite so many perks as a Gilded Knighthood.

With each of the other knightly factions—with the exception of the Knights of the Sword who are basically glorified mercenaries— one joins a knightly order. Each one comes with its own perks and downfalls, but they don't leave much room for individualism or forging your own fame. What you do, you do in the name of your knightly faction and likely with help. You don't see just one templar from the Brotherhood slaying a dragon; no, they always travel in groups of three or four.

I suppose if you like working as a team, then that's great for you.

If you want to become something, really become something then the Gilded Knights or the Knights of the Sword are the only two factions for you. And if you want to become something great then that rules out the Knights of the Sword.

A champion of the Gilded Order is a knight chosen by a fae lord, personally selected and granted a boon in return for their service. They serve one master, and they keep all the glory of their battles, but due to the limited number of fae lords out there who are willing to part with a piece of their magic in return for a loyal follower —they are very selective.

Which is where the academy comes in. It is more than just an elite training center like the other knightly academies. No, The Academy of the Gilded Knights is a competition. Only the best will graduate from it as a knight champion, the rest... well, I suppose they'll just have to reconsider their options. Anytime a fae lord decides that he or she needs a new knight, they go to stay at the academy. They look over the prospects and watch the contests, and then they choose the one who seems the worthiest to serve them.

I *will* be one of those knights chosen, and I'm going to be chosen by one of the more powerful high fae. I'll get a great magic as my boon and finally live down the shame of being born a low-magic fae.

Word is that the fae lord Menavilion is staying at the academy right now. He is looking for a knight, and I intend to be the one chosen. No matter his connections to Byron and his family, or the fact that Byron already wields magic from Menavillion. I'm not about to let that upstart steal another thing from me.

It's bad enough that he is the most powerful person in our village, despite the fact that *I'm* the only fae here. Or that he has claimed the hearts of everyone in the village. Or that my own friend Marvin is willing to stick up for him against me...

At least I'll get that knighthood and if Byron thinks that he has a chance in Skyshire of taking it from me, then he has another thing coming at him.

Marvin puffs out a breath, reaching up to wipe at his already perspiring forehead. I think he is wanting us to call a break, but the unfortunate fact of the matter is that we have only just reached the outskirts of the village, and the sun hasn't even fully risen yet.

We've barely even set out.

This is going to be such a long day... Poor Marvin, but if he wants a break then he is going to have to ask for it himself because if I speak up then Byron might think that I need it for myself, and I refuse to show weakness to the likes of him.

Maybe this will teach Marvin not to invite just anyone to travel with us, because if he hadn't, we could move at our own pace instead of the pace of that other person.

"So..." Marvin begins with a heavy exhale. "How is your grandfather?"

My mouth drops open and my foot stalls. The boy is fighting for his life over here to keep up with Byron's quick pace and he wants to make *small talk*?

Byron glances over at Marvin, his lips pressed into a thin line. "I wish that I could say he's doing better, but alas he didn't raise me to be a liar."

"That bad, huh?"

"I'm hoping he'll make it to winter," Byron's voice is tight as he speaks, and I swallow my own grief that begins to well in my throat, threatening to choke me. No matter what I think of his grandson, Tarus Coalbiter is a good man. One of the best there is.

His steady strength and quiet goodness have helped shape this village into the haven it became. I'm not so sure if the people of this town would have been so kind to a helpless stray like me if he hadn't extended me kindness first.

He's lived a hard life; his only child is a worthless drunk whose husband left her and he's had to basically raise his grandson... who grew up to be Byron. And yet, he's never allowed that to dim his positivity or cast a shadow on his goodness.

He's truly a remarkable individual, and I can't believe that he's so ill. It's true that he has been failing for some time as age does to all humans, but... why Tarus?

Why can death not distinguish between the sinner and the saint and take someone who more aptly deserves his fate?

"That's terrible, I'm so sorry," Marvin whispers, reaching out to rest a hand on Byron's arm. Byron's jaw works, but then he forces a smile although I can see the strain it causes.

I wonder why he is going to the academy this year if his grandfather's health is so frail, on top of being a wonderful man, he is also the man who raised him. If I had a person who raised me, and they were sick, I would stay by their side until they were either better or no longer with me.

As if sensing my unspoken question, he hikes the bag up higher on his shoulder. "I'm going to become a knight early. Before he goes. I know that's what he will want to see."

I tilt my head, perhaps it comes from knowing Byron my whole life, or maybe it's just because I don't trust him but... there's something he is keeping from us. I bite my tongue to keep from demanding that he tells us what it is. Marvin would just tell me that he's in mourning and he is allowed his privacy.

"How did your mother handle the news?" Marvin asks after a moment. Maybe he had the right idea about making small talk, it seems to have distracted him from his physical strain. His face is starting to look a little less purple.

"Oh, she doesn't know." Byron shakes his head. "She never sobered up enough for me to tell her. Farmer Trebbleweed will be keeping an eye on them both for me while I'm gone."

"Do you really think that you will gain your knighthood early?" I ask, finally speaking up. The Academy of the Gilded Knight houses prospective knights for a year, preparing them for a final tournament where they compete before the eyes of every fae looking for a prospective knight. They choose the knights they want and those that aren't picked... well, hopefully they'll have better luck in one of the other factions.

Sometimes though, if a knight shows especial promise a fae lord might swoop in and claim him or her before the tournament. If Byron intends to be a knight before his grandfather passes, then he will have to be one of those early picks. Winter is only a few months from now.

He shoots me a grin over his shoulder. "Why wouldn't I?"

I bristle at his words. Why wouldn't he indeed? After all, he is handsome, charming, and well-loved. All excellent qualities for a knight. On top of that, he has a powerful magic and is connected to a high fae already. What if Menavillion claims Byron as his champion as soon as he learns that he is looking for a patron? I won't even have a chance to try to prove myself before Menavillion has already taken a knight and left.

And I won't settle for any lesser lord. Menavillion is the one who gave Byron his magic. If I want magic as powerful as his, then I will need to get mine from the same source.

"What's that expression for, Lo?" Byron asks, his mouth twisting slightly. "You look like you swallowed a gnat."

I clench my teeth at the nickname. I've managed to get most everyone in the village to give up on calling me that. I'm already an orphan with no familial connections to back me, I was born with low-magic, and I'm a fae who was raised by humans. I cannot take a cutesy nickname to top it all off. How will anyone take me seriously if everyone insists on calling me *Lo*?

Dame Lo Brightbringer.

Oh, yes, it has *quite* the ring to it.

"Oh, Willow doesn't like being called—" Marvin begins, but he is cut off by the highest pitched voice that has ever had the misfortune of assaulting my sensitive ears.

My face twists with disgust as I turn to take in the only person from our village who I might actually hate more than Byron. *Gertrude Evertide.*

We are a small village, but there are enough young ladies my age to form a posse, and Gertrude is their leader. I think every girl in town might just be in love with Byron, which would explain why we don't actually get along, but Gertrude used her authority to put down the law.

Byron is *hers*. Any girl who says otherwise will quickly find frogs in her bed, worms in her water supply, and dead rats on her front step. Not that I actually care, let him have the little witch. They're both so despicable that it is almost as if they were made for each other.

Her blue eyes are welled up with tears that she won't actually let spill because they might make her cheeks look splotchy as she rushes down the road toward us. It's a strange run, the upper half of her body pivots as she goes like she's trying to make her hips sway suggestively while she runs. Not exactly the type of running that would save her life if she were to be chased by bearcat, but it is the type of running that gets Byron to stop and turn around.

His lips turn up in an amused smile as his eyes move up and down taking in her bouncing curls. "What's the matter, Gerda?"

"Don't you, 'what's the matter, Gerda,' *me*," she squeals, closing the distance between us. She nearly bowls me over in her haste to reach Byron. I step back, closer to Marvin as I brush off my tunic, wrinkling my nose as she latches onto his arm like a strangling vine.

She blinks up at him, her lower lip protruding almost comically. "You were going to leave without saying good-bye to me?"

"I said goodbye last night," Byron replies, baffled. "How many goodbyes do you need?"

"As many as it takes for you to say hello again."

"That doesn't even make any sense," I mutter with a snort. Apparently, I said it too loud because it draws both of their attention. I pull my lip in and reach up, tucking my hair around the point of my ear.

"Tell me you'll miss me while you are gone," she says as she turns her attention back to him.

"If that is what you want to hear," he says with a little smirk as he extradites his arm from her grasp. He flicks her nose. "You're such a silly girl, Gerda, how could I not miss you? It would be like missing my own shadow."

"Except your shadow doesn't worship the ground you walk on." I bite on my tongue as they both turn to me again. "Sorry, proceed."

Byron arches his brow. "Would you two like to go on ahead?"

"Oh, yes," Marvin exhales loudly, relief evident in his tone. "Come on, Willow."

I don't have to be told twice, especially with the way that Gertrude is currently gazing at the lower half of Byron's face. Knowing her and her womanly wiles, she won't be leaving without a goodbye kiss. And I for one don't intend to have to witness that.

I pick up the pace, hurrying up the slight incline of the dirt road that leads past the borders of our town and into the great unknown of the wide world. A land of cities and criminals where the humans are far more hardened than the good people of Woodsbury, a place where the wild fae live and monsters dwell. Out there are places so dangerous that humans haven't yet settled there.

And then there is Skyshire, the land of most fae. Floating cities that hang suspended above our own world.

Although, since I'm a fae I suppose that Skyshire is technically *my* world. I just somehow wound up in Commonweald. I'm certainly not the first fae to do so, just as there have been humans to settle in Skyshire. But still I wonder what my life would have been like if I had been raised in a city in the sky instead of a small human village in the middle of nowhere, where the only thing we have to boast in is a boy named Byron Coalbiter, a drunkard's son who was born with slightly impressive magic.

I may miss the slow life of a farming village, but I also know that I was made for so much more, my soul longs for adventure... and a little glory as well.

I inhale a deep breath, taking in the crisp morning air. Nearby I can hear a bird singing, until the sound is drowned out by pounding feet as Byron jogs up to us, a ridiculous grin on his face. "All right, I'm ready to be off. How about you?"

"Will you survive without your arm warmer?" I ask in a falsely sympathetic tone.

He waves away my words. "I'm sure I'll find many a lady to keep my arm warm at the academy. Until then... I suppose you could substitute. What do you say, Lo? My arm is getting a bit chilled already—"

I shove him before he can finish his sentence and stalk off, up the road.

Behind me, I hear his laughter and shake my head. This is going to be a long journey...

CHAPTER FOUR

N o one has any right being this cheerful on this hot of a day, and yet Byron persists.

I glare at his back, wondering why his shirt isn't soaked through with sweat before I reach up and wipe a bead of sweat off my own forehead. Marvin, I think, is going to die. However, either he has more pride than I gave him credit for, or he's worried that if he tries to talk, he will only speed up the dying process because he doesn't ask for a break.

Instead, he steadily plods along several paces behind me, his face redder than his hair, huffing and puffing the whole way.

If it weren't for my own pride, I'd ask Byron to stop for his sake. But knowing Byron, he won't believe me if I say it's for Marvin. He'll just take it as a sign of my weakness, and I've already determined to never appear weak in front of Byron Coalbiter. He has enough of a superiority complex as is without me adding to it.

Byron meanwhile is hiking far ahead of us, whistling like a songbird. If I thought Marvin would go through with it, I'd suggest we just let him wander ahead and we go find a different way to the Gilded Academy. After all, I'm sure that there are other roads that cut through this forest.

I'd take a deer path over Byron's company any day.

"Keep up, you two! I'd like to reach the Gilded Academy sometime this century," he calls over his shoulder, not even bothering to look back and ascertain that Marvin hasn't keeled over.

Byron skips on top of a large, flat rock, whistling the whole way. I eye the back of his shoulders, considering lobbing a rock at them and then pretending that some forest gremlin hopped out and did it. Perhaps Marvin is so preoccupied by breathing that he won't even notice that I was the one who threw it. He's a notorious do-gooder though and if he catches it he will tell Byron for sure.

He would snitch on his own grandmother if he knew she was telling a lie.

However, before I can make up my mind on whether I'm annoyed enough to actually resort to rock lobbing, Byron stops mid-tune. Those shoulders I was considering as a target stiffen. He stands there for a second before leaping off the rock and rushing forward, a sense of urgency in his steps that hadn't been there before.

I feel my heart begin pounding hard in my chest as I push myself to start running despite the fact that the heat and humidity feel so thick that it's almost like I'm having to swim through the air. Air clogs in my throat, but I force my feet to beat against the trampled earthen road that we've been following through this everglade forest.

As I race up the path Byron comes into view again. He's kneeling over something. Light glints off a metallic object and my foot twists as I realize that it's actually armor. Byron tilts his head to look at me, his hair falling down over his shoulder, blocking the face of the person from my view. His brows are drawn together in consternation as I stumble to a stop.

"Willow, quick, I need your hands."

I swallow hard and force myself to start walking again. I hurry to Byron's side and move around him, dropping to my knees as I take in the person lying on the forest floor.

He is a grizzled looking man about middle aged with long white gold hair bound at the nape of his neck in the same manner that Byron's hair is pulled back. A jagged scar running along the course of his face speaks of an experience in battle. His face is pale and beads of sweat form on his upper lip. His eyes are closed, but by the way that his face is pinched in pain it leads me to believe that he is not currently experiencing the sweet bliss of unconsciousness.

My eyes flick down his form, taking in the glittering armor he is adorned in. A knight. A templar from the carved insignia on his armor. His breastplate is rent, jagged bits of metal sticking up on either side. Byron has his hands stuffed in the crack of the armor, holding what appears to be a spare shirt in place. He turns to me, a droplet of sweat on the tip of his nose, wobbling as he moves his head.

"Willow, will you apply pressure to the wound?"

I swallow hard, pushing to my knees. My hands are shaking slightly as I slide them across the armor, brushing against Byron's hand as he pulls his out. My eyes widen as I take in how bloody his hands are. I can't really see the wound past his armor and the shirt held there, but the material is already warm and sticky, and a liquid seeps through to me.

Byron unclasps the canteen at his side and leans over the knight. "Sir?"

The knight opens his eyes, proving that I was right about him not being unconscious, and Byron presses the canteen to his lips. The man takes a greedy gulp releasing a sigh.

"You're hurt," Byron says, speaking in a soft tone that I must admit that I've never heard the boisterous black-smith's grandson ever use. "But it's okay, we can help you."

"No," the man moans, pressing his eyes shut. "I am beyond..." he wheezes, shaking his head. "You need to save her instead."

Byron ignores him, turning to me. He leans forward, ducking his head till his face is half buried in my hair. His forehead brushes against the tip of my pointed ear. "There's too much blood," he whispers in a low tone. "I'm going to have to cauterize the wound."

I nod, drawing in a shaky breath. "What do you need me to do?"

His mouth twists as he starts to unstrap the buckle of his belt. "Just get out of my way when I say."

I wrinkle my nose, but don't say anything due to the fact that he is currently removing his belt. My mouth drops open. Is now really the time to *disrobe*? I mean, I get that it is hot, but a man's life is in the balance. Not to mention the scandal...

Byron whips his belt around and leans over the man. "Bite on this, it's going to hurt a bit." He tries to place the leather belt between the man's lips, but the knight shakes his head, tilting away. "It's too late for me!" he snarls out. As he does so, I feel a liquid spurt against my wrist and hurriedly move my hands to apply pressure there. "You need to save the girl."

"Girl?" Byron asks, glancing at me as if I might be the girl in question. He looks like he is half considering slinging me over his shoulder and racing off all because of the vague warning of a knight who is very likely delirious with pain. "What girl?"

"The one I was to protect. Men-mena... she's the daughter of a high fae lord." He raises his hand, shakily pointing to a crevice barely visible between two large moss-covered rocks. "They took her through there. Please. You must get her back."

The knight grasps Byron by the front of his shirt and uses that to partially lift himself off the ground so that his face is only inches from Bryon's. I lose my grip on where I was trying to staunch the blood. "I swore... I swore..." he gasps.

"We'll save her," Byron says, reaching up slowly to grip the man's shoulders. "I promise."

"Good," the man gasps out. "I swore an oath to keep her safe." His eyes lock on something over Byron's head. I look over my shoulder half expecting to see a hawkhare perched in the trees, but the branches are devoid of any large predatory rabbits. My eyes flick down to see that Marvin has finally caught up. He is standing a short distance away, wringing his hands and looking pale.

I turn back around, just in time to see Byron gently lower the knight to the ground. He bows his head and I open my mouth to ask him why he isn't cauterizing the wound, but then he slowly raises his hand up and runs his hand down the man's face, pressing his eyelids shut.

I feel my eyes widen in horror as I struggle to process what I'm looking at.

"May you find peace in the Maker's embrace, Sir Knight," Byron mutters quietly, reciting a last rite over the fallen warrior.

CHAPTER FIVE

I almost wish that Byron would start whistling again so that I can at least pretend that nothing is amiss. But then, I suppose that no amount of pretending can actually change what happened.

There is a dead knight.

I draw in a shaky breath, struggling to keep from panicking as I rub my hands down my pants, forgetting that I have fresh blood all over them and staining one of my favorite tunics. Byron drops back on his heels as he stares blankly at me. However, I wonder if he even sees me.

"Guys... what was that?" Marvin squeaks. "What just happened? I was only a few paces behind you!"

Byron shakes his head. "I *found* him like this."

"But whatever happened to him happened recently," I say as I lean forward. I'm not entirely sure what I'm doing, my mind is buzzing, and my heart is racing and sweat mingles with the smudged blood on my palms. I lean forward, aimlessly plucking the wildflowers that lie in clusters in the tall grass on the edge of the path. I take the flowers and begin laying them around the knight in an arrangement.

"What are we going to do? Should we bury him?" Marvin squeaks.

"Yes. Perhaps." Byron shakes his head. "The knight said that someone—a girl—was in trouble. Perhaps she was his traveling companion. I think he would rather we see about rescuing her before we do anything with his body."

I shake my head, ripping up more wildflowers which I scatter across his chest. Perhaps if I bury him in flowers, I can hide the jagged hole in his armor in his chest. I know that doing so won't bring him back or make the empty hole in my own heart go away, and yet, I can't help but try. I want to run and hide, disguise the death, do anything but accept the truth that this man is dead. He's a complete stranger, and yet that doesn't change the finality of it all or how horrible it was.

This man died in the company of only strangers. We don't even know his name and yet we are the only ones who even know to mourn him right now. I sniff loudly, afraid to wipe at my face and leave a trail of blood there although it has mostly dried into a sticky paste on my hands. "If we leave him like this, the wild animals will feast on him."

"It's only a body now, Willow." Byron pushes to his feet. "If there is indeed a person in trouble, that's more important."

Marvin chuckles, nervously. It's a tad out of place in this moment, but I know that Marvin can't help it. When he gets nervous, he laughs. "We're forgetting that something killed this knight. If it killed a highly trained knight, then how do we stand a chance?"

"There's three of us," Byron says as he pats the sword at his side. "And we're knights-to-be ourselves. We aren't exactly helpless."

Byron, I know can hold his own in a fight, and I'm actually pretty flattered that he thinks I can too—indeed I'd like to believe that I could— but he is mad if he thinks of Marvin as anything other than a liability.

As if reading my thoughts, Marvin chuckles again. "That sounds like a completely solid plan that won't wind up with us dead on the side of the road just like this poor knight here."

Byron's mouth is pressed into a hard line. "What sort of knights would we be if we walked away from saving someone at the first sign of trouble?"

"The kind of knights who were forced to become ones because of their father's lofty expectations." Marvin glances between us, and his smile slides off his face. "But those aren't the kind of knights you are."

"You're the only one here *with* a father, Marvin," I say in a low tone. "Surely you could have come up with a more compelling argument than that. One that would actually *apply*."

"I'm nervous, Willow. You know that I can't think when I'm nervous!"

"Byron is right," I say with a shake of my head, even though that's honestly the last thing I ever wanted to hear come out of my mouth. I push to my feet, forcing my face to become impassive. I've had a lot of experience doing that. Spending my life living under other people's roofs and off their kindness I've seen a lot of things—families sometimes fight like wildcats behind the safety of their walls—and I've always had to keep a neutral party in family feuds for fear of getting thrown out on my bony tailbone. "We're knights-to-be, best we act like them. If someone is in danger, then who else will save them? We're here, we're capable." I side-eye Byron. Some of us are more capable than is rightly fair, but then I guess that we can't all be blacksmith's grandsons born with an unholy amount of magic. I swallow and rest my hands on my hips. "It's up to us."

"You know, you two are more similar than you think," Marvin says with a groan, pinching at the bridge of his nose. "You have savior complexes, the both of you."

I definitely don't appreciate Marvin telling me that I'm like Byron, and if I remember this insult when we're in a slightly less perilous situation then I'm going to give him an earful.

He releases a heavy groan and presses his eyes shut before jerking his head up in a nod. "You're going to be the death of me. Let's do this."

I nod and turn to Byron who has already moved to that crevice between the boulders. He has to stoop to enter. I race forward and slip into the shadows behind him. Immediately the air becomes cooler, and a slightly musty smell of moist dirt reaches my nose. I can make out Byron's silhouette highlighted by the sunlight that manages to trickle into the narrow cave, but it's impossible to tell how deep this cave is. For all I know it ends where the light does and I could wind up wandering into a wall.

Well, more likely Byron walks into the wall since he is in front... which would actually be kind of funny to watch. But I doubt it because there is no sign of this missing girl or whoever took her, and unless the dying knight was delusional with pain, which is always a possibility, they should be in here.

"Hey, could you provide some light?" Marvin's voice is a shaky whisper behind me.

To be honest, it's all I'm good for, but since my magic is actually coming in handy for once I decide not to complain. Instead, I lift my hand. Just as a small glow begins to appear above it, Byron raises his own hand. Sparks dance across his knuckles, blue light flicking across his fingers, moving like lightning and providing plenty of light. Unlike actual lightning it doesn't disappear after a second.

Instead, it gathers in an orb near his hand, far more violent than the one I would have created with the lights sparking and crackling with a dangerous energy. But also providing enough light that my own magic is rendered unnecessary.

I drop my hand in disgust.

See, this is what I hate about Byron. It isn't just that he has a powerful offensive magic that causes everyone to automatically respect him, it isn't even that he has that magic despite not having a drop of fae blood. It's that his power can do exactly what my magic can do and so much more.

He is not limited, and it isn't fair.

I can create light out of nothing. Which may seem exceptional until a person meets the boy who can make lightning. Bright, deadly, mesmerizing lightning. After that, who has any need for a little bobbing orb that emits a glow?

Byron's handheld lightning reveals that the cave extends much farther than I would have expected. It continues as far as the glow of Byron's light can go and then darkness enshrouds how much deeper it is. I can hear a faint dripping, and maybe if I strain my ears, I can hear what sounds like the low murmur of voices over the electrifying crackle of Byron's magic.

Byron glances back, his eyes flicking from me to Marvin standing behind me. "Why don't you guard the entrance?"

"What?" Marvin hisses.

"It won't do us any good if someone comes in behind us and traps us in here," Byron says, keeping his voice low. "Someone needs to stand lookout."

"I mean, if you think it will help..." despite Marvin's words, I can hear the stark relief in his voice.

Byron nods. "I do."

Marvin exhales. "Okay, I'll wait here."

We start forward again, but then Marvin grasps my arm. "Wait. What do I do if you don't come back?"

Byron swallows hard, I watch his throat bob before he turns around a smile plastered on his face. "We'll make it back."

"But if we don't, start praying and hope that for once the Maker hears you." I shrug. "And maybe run."

Not that running will help Marvin much. He likely wouldn't get very far or go very fast before he realizes that his body has forgotten how to breathe again. No, Marvin's best chance of survival is us. And our best chance of survival is not dying. The best way of going about doing that is likely by turning around right now, but unfortunately that isn't really an option so now I'm just going to have to hope for the best.

And maybe I should feel just a little honored that Byron didn't insist that I wait at the entrance with Marvin which likely means that he thinks I'll be less of a liability than him. Not that I care at all what Byron thinks of me. But still it feels kind of nice to feel recognized, even if it has to be Byron Coalbiter recognizing how much work and training I've put into my days. Or maybe I feel more pleased because it *is* Byron Coalbiter saying this and he is Woodsbury Grove's hero. I'm only it's orphan.

"Thank you for doing what you can to keep Marvin safe," I whisper as we slip deeper into the cave.

Byron glances back at me, the flickering light reflects in his eyes giving them a wild look. "You just... stay safe, okay. One dead knight is already too many."

I bite my lip and nod. "Yeah. You too."

Byron starts to turn but then he halts. I skid to a stop to keep from running into him. "Do you need my sword?"

I frown, considering refusing him as just as suddenly that warm feeling of thinking that he thinks my fighting skill are adequate fades, quickly to be replaced by frustration that he thinks I'll need a weapon.

But also, if it comes down to a fight then I *will* need a weapon and Byron's the blacksmith's son. He will have a proper blade, unlike the wooden sticks that I always practiced with in the woods beyond Woodsbury Grove.

I give a sharp nod, and he turns slightly, his shoulder brushing mine as he slides it out of its sheath. He passes it back to me, the bluish light of his magic casting his face into contrasting shadows as he presses his lips into a flat line. "Not that it will do much good if these tunnels don't widen."

Just as he finishes saying that I hear a voice, a sharply angry and distinctly feminine voice. "Unhand me! What is it you are doing? Is it not enough that you killed my guard, now you have to perform a *ritual* on me? What is *wrong* with you? Do you have any idea who I am?"

Byron and I both freeze, our eyes locking for a second before he turns and hurries down the cavern and I race to keep up with him.

Ahead the cavern appears to end, but as we draw closer, I spot the light bouncing into what appears to be another corridor that's around a sharp bend. Byron peers around the edge before he slams back, knocking into me and nearly skewering himself on his own sword. The light of his magic flickers out, and as I blink in the newfound darkness, I notice that there's a slight glow coming from around the bend. It's not exceptionally bright, but it's enough that I can at least see my hand when I hold it over my eyes and Byron' dark form.

There is a slight chant on the other side of the wall.

"Stop that! Whatever you are doing, stop that!"

"I counted half a dozen men," Byron whispers, tilting his head toward me. His hot breath whooshes over me. I blink several times as if that will remove the feeling as he shifts toward me, his shoulder pressing into mine. I notice that he leans down further. "There's a girl in the center, she seems to be in distress."

I nod to let him know that I got his message, but then I remember that it is dark as the underbelly of the world down here. And even though the top of my head brushes the bottom of his chin, he may still not have realized that I was nodding.

"I'll take care of the cultists; you save the girl."

I open my mouth to inform Byron that we don't actually know if they are cultists, but he is already moving away, and I decide that it isn't worth the argument. Especially when I step around the corner and take in what is going on beyond.

Just as Byron had counted, six men stand in a circle. At least, I assume they are men by their stature, but they are all hooded so it's really difficult to say. There are markings etched into the floor, they glow blue, providing the majority of light. One of the hooded men is holding a torch, but compared to the ethereal glow it seems far too dull and far too human.

In the center of the circle of the men, at the epicenter of the glowing symbols is a stake in the stone floor. A girl is tied to it, her hair and dress whips around her in a wind that does not exist in the rest of the cave.

It's an eerie scene.

I don't need to be a religious scholar or even a monk to recognize that there's something occult happening in these caves—and people wonder why the Maker turned his back on us...

Well, perhaps they should take up their abandonment issues with the people purposefully snubbing their noses at our creator and dabbling in the forbidden black magic.

The hoods appear to be blocking the cultist's peripheral vision because they don't notice us as we creep into the wider cavern. That is, they don't notice us until Byron plants his legs and holds out his hands on either side of him and conjures electricity from thin air. Sparks shoot across the room and dance around his hands before they shoot out toward the hooded figures.

"Cut her loose!"

I'm not sure why Byron felt the need to bark that order to me. Especially since I was already racing toward the girl, my head bent, and my sword held low in an attempt to avoid any stray sparks that might fly toward me. He isn't my boss, and I *don't* need to be told what to do. I'm perfectly capable of deciding my next course on my own.

I skid to a stop, jolting a bit when a hooded man takes a bolt of lightning through his chest. I swallow hard and with great difficulty, turn my focus on the girl, even if it means that I will have to trust Byron to guard my back from any cultists who he hasn't yet struck down.

Upon closer inspection, I realize that the girl in question is a fae, her pointed ears are visible over the curls of her tousled hair that is now half cascading from the bun she'd had it in. She is wearing a pale pink gown that is made of a light gauzy material that probably wasn't the best idea to travel in because now it looks like a dragon chewed it up and spit it back out.

I hold up my hand, grimacing a little when I see that my fingers are trembling and try my best to look reassuring. "Don't worry, we're going to get you out of here."

"What?" she yells and as she does so I realize that there is a rushing of wind near her that I couldn't hear in the rest of the cavern. I press my lips together before I decide that actions speak better than words anyway. I whip my sword up and make quick work at cutting through the binds holding her in place. She stumbles forward as the ropes holding her ankles to the stake release her. I jump to my feet, grabbing her hand, and yanking her into motion behind me.

I hear her gasp and feel wind whip at my hair behind me, but don't stop as I race toward Byron. I shove her toward him, he braces himself and manages to catch her.

The shock and frustration fades from her face as she takes in Byron, blinking rapidly as she starts to smile. Byron smiles right back, looking perfectly like the role of the suave savior. I roll my eyes and glance over my shoulder as I hear shouts. Hooded figures that Byron either missed, failed to kill, or came from a back cavern start to race forward.

"Close your eyes!" I bark.

Without waiting to see if Byron or our damsel comply, I throw my hands up, squeezing my own eyes shut. There is a flash of light so bright that I can make it out even through my eyelids. I blink them open, struggling past the spots, turning on my heel. I grab Byron's hand and yank him into motion behind me, hoping that he still has a hold of the damsel.

My power, for all the good that it did us, will only temporarily blind them. That's all light can do, really. We need to run before they get their bearings.

I race through the cavern, summoning a slight glow so that I don't entirely lose my way. Ahead I can make out Marvin's dark form by the mouth of the cavern.

"Run!" I shout, as I start to make out more shouts behind us.

Marvin stiffens and whips his head toward us. "Run!" I shout again since that boy is going to need as much of a head start as he can get.

He turns and takes off, not waiting for any further explanation, and we break out of the cavern, crashing into the forest and away from the cultists and their cave.

CHAPTER SIX

I have no idea where I'm going or where I'm heading. Somewhere along the way I lost Byron's sword, but hopefully we also lost the cultists back there as well. Byron and our damsel thunder ahead barely in sight. I have to keep slowing down to grab Marvin's hand and yank him along another several steps. I'm not sure how much longer I have before he completely collapses but given the purple coloring of his face I am going to bet that it won't be much longer.

As we go, the full gravity of the situation we were in begins to settle in. We attacked cultists, in their own lair. What if one of them had been a dark knight? What if they all had been? The Maker forsook the dark knights of the Fallen Order long before he left the rest of us, abandoning them even in death and now their bodies and souls are trapped forever in this mortal plain to slowly decay. We could have made immortal enemies today.

But surely, they don't know who we are, nor has there been any sign of pursuit. These woods are thick, we would hear them trying to come after us.

I whip my head around, my mouth halfway open, ready to tell Byron that perhaps we have run like the nether-hounds are on our tails long enough and we should take stock of our situation and figure out where we are, but my words die on my lips when I realize that Byron and our damsel is no longer there.

"Why that slimy son of a..." I begin, but just then I step forward and the ground shifts underneath me. I feel my eyes widen as I look down to realize that the foliage is not actually hard ground anymore. Instead, it appears that I'm standing on a mess of interlocking vines. Just as soon as I draw this conclusion, the vines shift apart and I pitch forward with a little squeak. I thrust my hands back, desperately grabbing at Marvin, but my fingers only just graze his shirtsleeve before I tumble forward into a mess of writhing vines below.

"Snakes! Snakes!" the damsel shrieks a minute too late to warn me of the impending danger.

Byron lifts his hand, his face scrunching with distaste as a vine coils around it. He has already sunk down to his chest in the vines. He glances at me as I wobble, struggling to keep my balance as the vines shift and *hiss* at me, trying to make enough of a gap for me to fall through.

"Careful," he says dryly. "It seems as if this portion of the forest is sentient, and quite possibly bloodthirsty."

I wrinkle my nose as I reach up, coiling my fingers into hair thin roots in the dirt beside me in a desperate attempt to keep above the vines that are currently trying to swallow me. The same way they are slowly sinking Byron lower and lower.

I've read that portions of some forests have developed a taste for blood and the trees and plants have created traps for small animals to fall prey to, but I never actually imagined a feral part of the forest could be this close to Woodsbury.

But then, I also never imagined that there was a cave full of cultists just down the forest road.

"Thanks for the warning," I retort sharply.

The corner of Byron's mouth turns up in a smile that is really not appropriate given the situation. "Don't mention it."

"Help me!" the damsel screams in a voice that is so shrill it almost makes Gertrude's tone seem less grating. Almost.

Byron and I both turn to see the damsel neck deep in the vines. Only her face and a single hand are above the writhing green mass and even those are sinking far quicker than I would like. After all, we did go through a lot of trouble to save her just to lose her to sentient vines.

"Stop struggling, Princess. They can probably sense fear and desperation." He grunts a little and holds out his hand, grasping hers before it can disappear below the surface forever. "Here."

She desperately grasps at his hand, her eyes wide and frantic. A bit how I'm feeling right now but I'm not about to let my eyes betray me.

Marvin peeks his head over the edge. "Are you all right?"

"We're about to be swallowed alive by vines," I yell up. "How do you think that I'm doing?"

Marvin's mouth twists. "What should I do? Should I run back to town and get some help?"

"That's a lovely idea," Byron replies dryly. "At least then you'll have help pulling our corpses out of here."

I roll my eyes at his sharp retort despite the fact that I just snapped at Marvin myself. Marvin doesn't think well under pressure, we can't expect a miracle from him. There are no saints here.

I grit my teeth and hold up my hand. "Can you reach me?"

Marvin looks a little gray, but he manages a nod and lowers his hand until our two clasp. I start to hoist myself up, wondering if I happened to pack some rope in my satchel, but then suddenly I feel a hand grasp my leg. A bit too high for my comfort. I whip my head around, a sharp retort rising when I realize that it's Byron who has a hold of me. However, that dies on my lips when I see that he isn't looking at me to even see where he grabbed me. Instead, he is shaking out his foot, to dislodge a vine while simultaneously trying to pull the damsel out of the thick of the vines coiling around her.

"What are you doing?" I manage to get out. Almost civilly too. Which is quite a feat considering that his hand is currently resting in a place that his hand should *never* be.

"Try to hang onto to Marvin, we're going to need to climb out and then we'll pull you up."

"You mean you're going to climb up me?" I demand. "I'm not a ladder, you know." Forget my thigh, there are a lot of places I don't want Byron touching. My whole body for one.

Byron offers me a lopsided smile. "Could have fooled me, you make a very attractive ladder though so you can wipe that expression off your face."

"And I'm just supposed to hang here until you get up?" My arm starts trembling at just the thought. I feel a bead of sweat form on the bridge of my nose.

Marvin grunts, reminding me that he is also having to hold us all up. But at least he gets to lie on his stomach and not have to be balanced on writhing vines. "Come on, Willow, you said you had broad shoulders earlier. Use them," he says, his tone low and strained.

Byron chokes on a laugh, and I glare down at him where he is hanging onto my waistline. "Do you find this funny?"

"Sorry, just trying to wonder what drove you to think that you had broad shoulders."

We can't all be blacksmiths by trade, Byron. I narrow my eyes at him, but that turns into a wince when the damsel digs her heel into my calf as Byron helps to give her a hand up. I grit my teeth and press my eyes shut.

This is honestly just humiliating. The damsel's foot kicks my face as she shimmies up. I feel Marvin's grip loosen a little bit as he gets his first view of her.

"H—hello," he stutters shyly.

I groan and roll my eyes. Now is *not* the time for him to get a crush.

She finishes making her way up me and pulls herself up onto the ledge above. "I nearly died, do not *hello* me!"

I work to tighten my hand around Marvin but either his palm is sweating, or my palm is sweating... or perhaps both our palms are sweating, because I find my fingers starting to slide through his. "Marvin, I'm slipping!"

Just as the words are out of my mouth, I lose my grip on him and tumble backwards. I don't know if Byron was trying to catch me or if he had just been standing there but the end result is still the same. Us landing in a mess of tangled writhing vines, me on top, him on the bottom. My chin hitting his bony collar so hard I nearly bite my own tongue off.

Byron groans and slowly lifts his head up so that he is looking at me. "Ow, Lo, get off."

I roll my eyes. "My name isn't Lo," I grind out as I struggle to get up. I gasp out as I feel a vine coil around my waist holding me to him.

He snorts. "Uh... yes, it is. That's what I've called you for your whole life."

I press my elbow into his chest, I swear it's only because I'm trying to get my bearing, but I can't lie and say that the little grunt he gives isn't at all satisfactory. "And I've called you arrogant toadstool your whole life. That doesn't make it your name."

"Get off me. Or are you seriously going to get the both of us crushed to death out of pettiness?"

I narrow my eyes. Pettiness? I would never allow my hatred of Byron to actually endanger either of our lives. Does he think I would? "I'm *stuck*, Byron, but it's nice to see that this is your opinion of me."

His eyes flash as a vine creeps up, twining around his cheekbone. "Oh, as if you don't have a worse one of me."

"Guys!" Marvin calls.

"Stay out of this, Marvin," Byron and I snap at the same time.

"Well, that's it then. I'm not saying anything nice at your funeral."

I shake my head as I begin wriggling, trying to see if I can make it out from underneath the vine. I twist my hips as I try to rotate my body enough to snag the knife attached at the sheath in my belt. It's a pocket knife, one that was actually given to me by Byron's grandfather. I wonder if old Tarus ever saw me using it to try to free myself and his grandson from sentient plants. I nearly drop it when the vine tightens around me, pressing me more tightly into Byron.

"What *are* you doing?"

"Trying to save both of our lives," I grind out.

He smirks, his irritation from earlier fading away. He snaps his teeth at a vine that is trying to wind near his mouth before saying, "Oh, I thought that you were going to make up after our fight."

I just barely stop myself from rolling my eyes. "Two things you should already know about me, Byron Coalbiter. I do *not* make up that quickly, I need to stew in it like a bog monster in the swamps."

I bite on the edge of my lip, focusing on the constricting vine that is now threatening to crush the bones of my leg.

"And two?" Byron prompts after a moment.

Finally, the knife snaps through and the vine flails and falls away with a muted shrieking hiss. I push to my feet, blowing a stray strand of hair that has fallen into my face away and reach down grasping Byron by the belt strapped across the front of his tunic and help hoist him to his feet, out of the hold of the vines that had nearly swallowed him into the pit. I glare up at him, taking in his gaze that is so blue it would make the sky jealous before I step away with a growl. "Two is that I would *never* apologize to the likes of you."

I turn away with a huff, leaving Byron looking a little bewildered. But it isn't my fault if he has yet to realize our rivalry. It started when we were children and has lasted most of our lives. It's his own stubborn obtuseness that would refuse to see that it's been me or him from the start.

There can be no peace.

No truce.

No playing nice.

All of my life he has shown me up, and one of these days, I'm planning on returning the favor. If he isn't expecting it, it just makes it that much easier for me.

I trip over a vine but manage to catch myself on the dirt wall that lines the pit. I'm eyeing it for grooves I can use to climb up. I could always have Marvin try to pull me up but I'm not sure if I trust his upper body strength or his sweaty palms for the task.

And the last thing I want is to wind up in a situation where I'm lying on top of Byron again held in place by evil vines.

I reach up, to grasp a portion of stringy root that fortunately doesn't look sentient when suddenly warm hands envelop my hips and my feet are off the ground. I kick my legs as my hand flies to the hands on my waist and I turn a glare down at Byron.

"What are you *doing*?" I hiss, but then I immediately regret it when I realize that I'm just mimicking what he said earlier.

"Trying to save both our lives." I can hear the smile in his voice. "Hold still, silly, I'm only giving you a boost." With a grunt, Byron lifts me higher until I'm able to grasp the edge of the pit. My arms shake a little as I pull myself up, but with Byron shoving me up from below, and Marvin rushing forward and grasping my arms, I manage to get up.

Even the damsel helps a little bit by standing off to the side wringing her hands and looking worried.

Once I'm on the ledge I turn around and lie on my stomach lowering my hand to Byron.

He stops mid reaching for a clump of dirt for purchase as he eyes my hand suspiciously. "You aren't going to drop me, are you?"

"At least not by accident," I reply dryly.

Marvin lies down next to me and brings his hand down. "It's okay we got you."

Byron presses his lips together, but a vine begins winding around his ankle. He shakes it off and jumps up, finally grasping our proffered hands and allowing us to pull him out of the pit.

CHAPTER SEVEN

I will be glad to leave behind that pit of vines. This whole forest really. I'm ready to make it to the Academy. While I've never actually been to Skyshire, and the idea of whole cities hanging suspended in the clouds boggles my mind, it's technically the land of the fae and Commonweald down here is the home of the mortals.

I was born for Skyshire.

Or maybe I'm exactly where I should be, after all, I may be a fae, but what place does a low-magic fae have amongst high lords?

"Is everyone unhurt?" Marvin calls, turning in a small circle as he takes us all in. I don't know what he plans to do if we say that we are wounded. None of us here are paladins who are blessed with powerful healing abilities.

If there were a paladin here then that templar wouldn't have died, but alas it seems all the holy servants are busy elsewhere. Fitting. Just like their Maker.

I reach down, rubbing at an area where the vine tore through my pants leg. My skin is a little red underneath, but what makes me the most upset is the tear. I don't have nearly enough clothes that I can afford going around tearing them up.

I straighten, frowning when I see Byron is watching me. "What?" I demand.

He blinks. "Just making sure that you're all right."

"As all right as I can be all things considered," I reply with a shrug. "You?"

"I suppose I don't have much of a right to complain considering a man lost his life today. I'm far better off than he is now."

"He's in the arms of the Maker now," Marvin says in a low tone. He is kneeling next to the girl and appears to be fussing on a light scrape on her wrist.

I glance at Byron, wondering his opinion on the matter. The way I see it, a lot of people either cherish and revere the Maker or have major abandonment issues from him. There is seldom an in between and what does exist is usually walked by the fae who believe themselves superior to needing a god to guard their steps.

"You're assuming that he found the Maker," Byron says sharply, which I suppose answers my question. He is in the abandonment issues department. "But I hope wherever he wound up he is at peace now."

"Not that he deserves it," the damsel says with a loud sniff and drawing our surprised glances her way. "The man failed in his duty and went off and died when I needed him. I could have been killed!"

"And yet here you are. Alive and complaining and he's bled out beside a cave likely to become the meal of a bear... assuming the cultists don't desecrate his body in one of their rituals. So, I don't think that you really have a right to complain," I reply sharply.

"It was his *duty* to protect me. His dying neglected that duty."

I fold my arms as I stare her down. "How inconsiderate of him."

Byron cuts me a hard look. "You're not helping," he whispers.

I'm not entirely sure what I'm supposed to be helping so I settle for just glaring right back.

Marvin finishes tying off a bandage around the girl's wrist. "Can you tell us your name?"

"Indeed, I am Istaria Everfair." She replies primly, smoothing out her skirts although a second later the wind that seems to exist only where she is begins blowing again.

"This definitely looks like the works of dark magic," Marvin says leaning toward her. He lifts a hand as if to touch the strand of hair that seems to be floating on its own.

Istaria moves back, her perfectly straight little nose wrinkling. "Oh really? Was it that occult ritual that gave it away?"

"Why were those cultists after you, do you think?" Marvin asks gently, not seeming to be bothered at all by her sharp words.

She sniffs loudly, raising a trembling hand to her face. I think a better question would be to ask what they were doing to her. Her hair and clothes are still blowing as if affected by wind, but the rest of the forest is still. It's somewhat unsettling to behold. "I have no idea. I was simply traveling to meet my betrothed when they attacked us, killed my guard, and dragged me into their lair. I wasn't there for too long before you arrived."

"Your.... Betrothed?" Marvin asks, choking on his words. It's the only thing that she has said that actually seems to have phased him. Odd considering all the other utter nonsense that has come from her.

72

She nods once, glancing down at her nails, which are of course perfectly long and rounded. "I am to marry Lord Menavillion."

This causes me to choke. "Lord Menavillion?"

She looks up, narrowing her eyes. "Is there a reason that you two keep repeating everything I say?"

Byron leans closer to her, resting his forearm on his knee. "I believe they're just surprised. You see, my family actually has had dealings with Lord Menavillion in the past. I was traveling to the Gilded Academy in the hopes of becoming one of his knights, actually."

I stiffen at Byron's words. They land only a little gentler than a physical blow. I knew that Byron was aiming for Menavillion. With his history with the fae, it wouldn't make sense for him to try to become the knight of a different high lord. Yet hearing my suspicions confirmed only serves to make me feel as if I've been stabbed in the stomach. And the knife was then twisted.

I can no longer tell myself that I am just being paranoid, or try to convince myself that Byron is anything other than he has ever been.

He's my rival. I slide my gaze to him. He's looking at Istaria, but seems to sense my eyes on him because he looks up. We stare at each other as a long second as I find myself trapped by his shockingly blue orbs. Blue, just like the lightning he wields. Looking into his eyes reminds me of why I hate him.

He's effortlessly perfect at everything, even possessing magic.

"We're all heading to the Gilded Academy," Marvin hurriedly adds. He's red like a flower and perspiring despite the fact that the heat has finally broken and it's starting to grow cool here. "I mean, I'm not actually trying to serve the High Lord Menavillion, but I am looking to become a gilded knight."

"You? A gilded knight?" She raises her hand as she giggles slightly. "I suppose that's what the academy is for after all, to sort out unworthy candidates."

Marvin smiles sheepishly, chuckling a little bit. I feel my eyebrows rise; does he not realize that she was insulting him?

Her eyes slide to me. "And the fae? What is one of her kind doing here in the company of humans?"

"She's our friend," Marvin says.

"She's traveling to the academy as well," Byron replies evenly.

"Oh, she's one of *those* fae." Her eyes flick down my form. I resist the urge to squirm under her scrutiny. I don't need to ask what she means by *those* fae. There are the fae that live in Skyshire, in their castles in the sky with their powerful magic, locked in bitter conflicts and using humans as their pawns and then there are fae that walk the ground of Commonweald, raised amongst humans, whose blood is mingled with their own. To the pureblo800ed fae, the mixed bloods of Commonweald are nearly as bad as humans even though we now make up the majority of the fae. Still, I can tell what type of fae this girl is as she leans away from me as if she might catch my inferiority. "Low-magic, are we?"

I push to my feet, dusting myself off, although it will likely take much more than the cursory pat to rid myself of the dirt and grime now covering my pants and tunic. "We should be off. We're going to run out of daylight, and if we linger much longer, we'll give the cultists more than ample time to catch up."

Byron nods, pushing to his feet. "You're right."

Marvin holds out a hand to Istaria. "My lady, if you will allow us, we will bring you to the academy safely."

"Of course, you will," she says frowning at his hand, but she accepts it anyway. "What sort of knights to be would you be if you left me here on my own?"

What sort of knights indeed?

Probably not very good ones, but I sure as blazes would feel better if I tossed her into that vine pit and left her to her pompous attitude to try to get herself out.

But then I remember that she's a pureblooded fae which likely makes her more powerful than any of us, even Byron. Which would make her far too powerful an enemy to make, even if I weren't trying to win the patronage of her betrothed.

Although if I were to serve Menavillion and he marry her... that would make her my lady.

Which is almost too much an idea to bear even with the promise of a more powerful magic.

CHAPTER EIGHT

M arvin and Istaria start walking, but Byron is just standing there, angled toward me, watching me with those unsettling blue eyes that would fit a fae better than a human. I wonder if he hit his head in our escapade and that's why he hasn't picked up that we are moving forward again. Marvin and Istaria are already starting to get a lead on us. Marvin is prattling on, something about turnips and his father's farm being the foremost producer of the root vegetable on this side of Commonweald.

But Byron is just standing there, letting them leave us behind and looking at me in a way that makes me a little uncomfortable. Although, I'm not entirely sure why except that the expression on his face reminds me a bit of his grandfather.

Old man Coalbiter has a way of looking all the way to your soul, and that reminder that Byron is his grandson serves to make me feel a little guilty for openly despising him. Whatever I feel toward Byron, I do truly respect and look up to the grandfather.

Byron smiles slightly, it's a slow hesitant smile as he rests his hands on his slim hips. "Hey, uh, Lo. I just wanted to address what happened earlier."

I arch my brow.

"I'm sorry about those unkind things I said to you while we were in the vine pit. It was a high stress situation." He holds up his hands as if expecting me to interject something. "Not that it excuses me. I didn't mean any of that. I don't think that you actually hate me."

Now both my eyebrows have shot up. He doesn't? I must not have made myself very clear then.

He holds out his hand as if expecting me to clasp it. "So... friends?"

"We've never been friends, Byron Coalbiter," I say stiffly as I brush past him, his outstretched hand dropping. It brushes my arm as it does so, but I don't look back.

I can feel his eyes trailing along my back, but I don't dare turn around and risk seeing his hurt expression.

I flex my fingers, almost feeling the imprint of that hand clasp I should have accepted, but it would have changed nothing.

We both want the same thing, something that only one of us will be able to walk away with.

We aren't friends, never have been, and now we can never be. It would be a lie to say otherwise.

And there are terrible consequences for fae who lie.

I stride forward, trying to ignore the muttered, "*Women*," from behind me. I raise my head higher as I pass Marvin and Istaria. I've spent enough time tramping through woods growing up. They were where I sought sanctuary when I needed some time to myself in the past. It's now almost instinctual to know which way is north, even though the sun is blocked out by the branches over-head.

At least, I certainly hope that I've not allowed myself to become turned around, otherwise I will probably find some ditch and die of embarrassment. After the vine pit, I only have so much dignity left, and I'd like to hold on to it in front of the future Lady Menavillion.

Behind me, I can hear my companions begin to start talking as time passes and some of the tension eases as it becomes less and less likely that the cultists will catch up to us.

We will make it to our destination soon enough and after that, we will be safe. But I'll still have to face the task of convincing Lord Menavillion to choose me as his knight over Byron, a man who already has his magic running through his veins. Fae are partial like that. I'm connected to my magic, little enough that I have. If I granted a portion of it to someone, I would sure as blazes want to keep it close.

I'm sure that even high fae like Menavillion, who have more than enough magic, feel the same way even if they're more than happy enough to bargain away bits of their magic in return for favors. It's a small enough price to pay, but it's still a price to be paid. A shrewd fae like Menavillion will probably leap at the opportunity to reclaim that magic back even if it is in the form of Byron's knighthood.

I need to convince him that I'm the better option. Somehow...

"Have you met your betrothed?" I hear Byron ask behind me.

"Have you met him?" Istaria asks although her voice lacks the bitter edge I have heard her use when speaking to Marvin or me.

"No, but I've certainly heard many things about him." Byron sighs, and I dare a glance over my shoulder, but he simply shrugs. "Will you answer my question now?"

"Of course, I have met Lord Menavillion. As a fellow high fae, we walk in many of the same circles. I am used to the company of my peers not whatever ragtag group this might be." I start to look over my shoulder to glower at her, but then my foot slips on the bark of a root, and I decide to keep my focus up front.

"And do you know Menavillion's guards? I assume he keeps them near him."

"What do mere knights matter to the likes of me?" she asks.

"Just... trying to make conversation." There is something in Byron's voice, a tightness that makes me ponder if he is speaking truthfully. If he was actually trying to make conversation, then why would he press so hard about a vague subject?

Is he trying to figure out what life as a knight champion will hold in store for him? I hope he doesn't expect to rub elbows with the high fae, even find one to be his bride and elevate his status in the world.

He might be something back at Woodsbury Grove, but here he is just a blacksmith's son with slightly higher than par magic. In Skyshire, he would simply be a knight sworn in service of a high fae, his worth relying on the patron he serves.

I start to feel a smile come across my face. If he is entering this academy with delusions of grandeur, then it will be my utmost honor to pop those delusions and send him crashing right back down to Commonweald where he belongs.

Perhaps it is not Menavillion that I need to convince of my worth, but Byron I need to remind of his own self-importance. After all, the life of servitude that comes as a knight—even an esteemed knight champion— is no life for a blacksmith's grandson who was born with too much magic, too pretty of a face, and too much ego.

I turn the idea through my mind, trying to figure out how to go about my plan, but ahead the trees clear and as I get my first glimpse of the world beyond my mind clears of all thoughts save for awe.

Woodsbury Grove is a beautiful little town, the cottages are quant and for the most part well-tended. The people are friendly. Trees are scattered throughout the village, growing between houses and behind the smithy. During Autumn, they are brilliantly arrayed in colors and during spring they harbor the fragile blooms of new life.

Any walls we have are short, carved out of stone with moss growing out of it. Their purpose is to guard turnips and keep cows out of our gardens.

Most people in Woodsbury Grove have spent their whole lives there. They were born there, and they fully intend to die there.

It's a beautiful little town, and it's an isolated town. Most people living there see no need for life outside of the grove. It's as if it is a world all its own and for my whole life it was *my* world.

And so, while I have heard of cities and castles suspended in the sky, of knights and monsters I never actually experienced any of it. It was like a fairytale to me. One that I knew was real, but I'm not entirely sure if I believed it until now.

Past the tree line, there's a beautiful lake, mist rises off it. Its waters are dark, cast into shadow by the massive island floating above it.

My mouth drops open as I tilt my head back trying to take in the structure. It hangs suspended in the air as if it doesn't way tons. The sky is barely visible past the rocks, and underneath it is so dark that it looks almost as if it is night on the lake.

An anchor runs from the floating island, disappearing into the ground near a clustering of shacks. A human village that is built on the anchor line of the fae city is visible to the right along the lake. Likely, they are there to make a profit from everyone trying to enter Skyshire and to thrive off the fae's prosperity.

It's hard to imagine that this existed only a day's walk through the thick woods from the sleepy little town I was raised in. All my life it was just within my reach, and yet, I never ventured forth to claim it. I'm sure there's a metaphor or a lesson to be learned somewhere in there about a world of infinite possibilities and us being the ones to sell ourselves short, but it is lost on me.

A lot of things are lost on me as I take in the massive structure floating above the lake. The bottom looks almost like a cliff face, jagged rocks that narrow into a point at the bottom. Over the grassy edge at the top of the floating island I can make out spires and turrets that are only just visible because of their height.

Up there is a fae city. Up there is Skyshire. It's where I belong and once I'm a gilded knight I'll finally rejoin my people. Not as some low-magic fae, but as a fae with powers in my own right. The magic I gain from my knighthood will be everything. It will be an inheritance for my children, my dowry for my future husband, and my invitation to finally start living life as a fae rather than living like one of the humans I was raised by.

CHAPTER NINE

The human village reminds me a little of Woodsbury Grove except it is smellier, wetter, and dirtier. So, all in all, not very much like my hometown, but I have nothing else to compare it to.

The air reeks of fish and dampness, two things that I didn't realize that air could smell like. The streets are made of mud with deep divots running through them that were likely made by wagon tracks. Tiny rivers of water sit in the divots, waiting for you to slip into them and soak your boots.

No one offers us kind smiles as we make our way through. No one greets us at all. We're just a group of strangers passing through their lake town, and strangers we shall remain. I suppose that with them being a transport hub that leads into a portion of Skyshire they are used to strangers, unlike the people of Woodsbury Grove who would flock to meet any outsider.

With how quiet our life was, it didn't take much to impress us. After all, most everyone thought that Byron was something. The people here that do happen to gaze upon us do so with the heavy-lidded gaze of unimpressed wariness.

Children race barefoot in the mud. I glance at my companions to see Byron looking at them with sad eyes. "Grandfather always said that the world of the fae casts a rot on humanity because it makes us crave what we can never have." He slides his gaze to me and some of the sadness clears as he twists his mouth in a remorseful smile. "He didn't mean that about you, of course, Lo. He meant it about their magic and glamourous cities in the skies and how that morals will trade just about anything to have those things for themselves."

I arch a brow. "And yet you're trying to become a knight to impress him. You know the Academy of the Gilded Knights was founded by a fae, right?" Not just any fae, a high fae. The most powerful, pureblooded fae there are. There are knightly orders that were founded by humans, and while there is no longer a distinction between human or fae in who can join, if it bothers his grandfather so much it makes me wonder why he chose this knightly order out of all the ones available.

Byron's mouth pinches. "I know. Trust me, I wouldn't be bargaining with any fae if I had a choice."

He turns away as if his words didn't just fill me with more questions. What does he mean that he doesn't have a choice? He's making it sound like he would rather just stay and be a blacksmith in Woodsbury Grove but that there is something other than his own vain ambitions driving him to become a knight champion.

Mud splashes under my boot as I quicken my pace. I reach out my hand to tap Byron on the arm, my question forming on the tip of my tongue. But before I can voice it, he reaches a building at the edge of the village. It is built right on the lake, directly next to the massive anchor. Set up next to the anchor is some sort of pulley mechanism with a wooden box that has railings next to it.

"Excuse me," Byron says, not noticing the hand that is half raised to tap him on his shoulder. I nibble on my lip, dropping my hand and tucking it behind my back before anyone notices my failed attempt to get Byron's attention. I dart a glance at Marvin, but he is staring at Istaria, in fact I don't know if he has really taken his eyes off her since we met her. Istaria is looking with some trepidation at the wooden contraption.

The man who Byron greeted looks up. He is wearing a ratty cloak that looks like it has never been washed, his hair hangs around his head in dark stringy waves. His face has a weathered look to it that leads me to believe that he spent many of his days in the sun, not in this small village that has been thrown into the shadow of the floating city above. His eyes flick across our group before he smiles, revealing several rotting teeth. "Looking to have a ride up to the city above?" he asks, his voice is low and gravely. "Well, you've come to the right place. I'm the ferryman."

"We want to go up, not across the lake," I say, stepping up beside Byron. I open my mouth once again to ask my question, but the ferryman cuts me off.

"The city up there is where I'll ferry you." He points up. He steps out to the right and toward the wooden structure, patting it so hard it creaks. "You just ride this up and up, and you'll find yourself in the city of the fae."

"*Ride*? *That*?" I sputter as I look over the wooden contraption. I can see now why Istaria had such a look of distaste directed at it. I hear Marvin swallow hard, but other than a little squeak he doesn't mention that he's terrified of heights. We both knew that this was coming up when we set out to attend the Academy of the Gilded Knight, after all, it's situated in the sky. In Skyshire, where we are headed, a fear of heights is impractical.

Byron races past me, splattering my boots and leggings with mud as he goes before he jumps into the wooden wagon. It is held about an inch above the ground, suspended by thick ropes—that aren't nearly thick enough to consider holding my weight— that are tied together into a complex mix of knots and pulleys. The ferry sways under his new weight.

"Come on, Lo, don't tell me that you are afraid."

I cross my arms. "I'm fearless, but that doesn't mean that I'm keen on dying."

He grins as he reaches out to brace his hand on the railing that goes around the majority of the flat cart. "Cowardice is so unappealing on you."

I grit my teeth and ball my fist striding forward and stepping onto the ferry. I glare up at Byron who just continues to smirk at me. "You can't scare me, Byron Coalbiter."

His eyes light up with a challenge that tells me that perhaps I should have kept my mouth shut. Now, he's probably going to start shaking the ferry when we're halfway up which will lead to the ropes snapping and then we'll all fall to our deaths. And all because I can't back down from a challenge.

As if sensing my thoughts, Marvin sighs loudly behind me, and I feel the platform dip slightly under his weight as he moves on behind me. "If we die, at least, we'll all die together."

I'm not entirely sure what about that thought is comforting, but Byron ignores him and holds his hand out to Istaria. "Are you coming, princess?"

She purses her lips but accepts his hand and allows him to help her up. I move to the other side of the ferry partly to make more room for her and partly because I'm a little worried that it will capsize from an uneven weight distribution.

"Four heads are forty crowns."

I feel my eyes bug out of my head. "That's ridiculous."

He shrugs. "You won't find another way to get up to that city anytime soon, or for any cheaper."

"That's extortion."

"That's business," Byron says dryly. "Isn't it my friend?"

The man shrugs again.

Marvin holds up his hand, reaching into his pouch. "Don't worry, I can handle this. I might not be much good for anything, but at least my father has money."

"Nonsense, Marvin, you're plenty useful," I say. I'd rest my hand on his shoulder, but I don't want to move toward him and risk putting too much weight on one side of the ferry. Instead, I settle for leaning back against the railing.

It digs into my lower back, but I take comfort in it being there.

"Yeah, for one he can afford to get us places." Byron smacks his arm. "Thanks for this."

Marvin shrugs. "Think nothing of it."

Byron will probably do just that. I look over to Istaria to see her opinion on the matter, but she is simply staring up at the city over our heads longingly. "I cannot wait to return to some semblance of civilization again."

I'd count this rickety little village as some semblance of civilization, but I suppose that I haven't been where she has or witnessed the grand halls that she has.

The ferryman nods at whatever Marvin puts into his hand before he snaps a gate shut. "It will be a slow but steady progression; I suggest you not fall out because I'm charging to clean up whatever messes you make as well."

I open my mouth to ask what he is going to use to pull us up since I doubt it will be his skinny arms, but just then I catch sight of some movement behind the ferryman's house. One end of rope disappears over there and seems to be wrapped around a cog built into the ground. Tethered to it are Wildenbeasts, large reptilian omnivore creatures. They're usually gentle, so much so that they can be used as beast of labor, but they also have been known to eat enough small animals and fish that I wouldn't trust any around a child. The kid might just disappear...

Still, they are very powerful creatures and normally good natured, known to build a very dependent relationship to the humans that feed them, so I suppose that it makes sense that these would be the creatures to be working the pully.

The ferryman steps toward them, clicking his tongue, and they begin pacing around the wheel, pushing on its ends forcing it to move. With a groan, the platform lifts off the ground. I widen my stance, grasping the ropes desperately as we begin our slow ascent into Skyshire, the place where I very well could have been born. It's certainly where I plan on spending the rest of my life, and yet it's a world I have also never known.

I've only read about it, and I know that books can sometimes lie.

After all, they say that the Maker loves us, that all fae are powerful creatures, and storybooks paint people like Byron into heroes.

CHAPTER TEN

I can't help it; I'm gaping by the time the ferry makes it to the end of the rope. Riding up, I'd felt a little nauseous and had spent most of my time focusing on breathing and *not* looking down to the steep drop that would surely spell my doom. But now that I have made it to the top and am able to step out on firm ground, my worry and unease has melted away replaced only by awe.

Skyshire.

In all my dreams I'd never imagined it half this resplendent.

Grand buildings line streets that are paved with a type of stone that glimmers in the sunlight, which is brilliantly bright now that we are out from under the shadows of the floating city. The air is crisp and clear, and the clouds are so close that it almost feels like I could reach up and touch them.

"Wow," Byron breathes. He turns back to us, his eyes glittering as he grins. "Have you ever seen anything so beautiful?"

"I don't think so," I whisper, but for some reason I can't seem to turn my gaze from him and the way the wind whips up his hair and sends it flying around his face. His eyes, I notice are the exact shade of the sky and for just a moment, I can see why all the girls of Woodsbury would fall for him.

"I saw something more beautiful," Marvin says, finally pulling my gaze away from Byron. "I met her this afternoon."

I look up to Istaria who sniffs loudly at Marvin's comment. Her hair and skirts are being whipped around, but in the opposite direction of the wind. Hopefully when we reach the academy and her betrothed, we'll be able to figure out what sort of dark magic has been used on her. She reaches up to tuck a strand of hair behind her ear but in a second it flies free and begins floating around her face again.

She doesn't look amused. Or impressed. "This city is too close to the humans, look at how their architecture has ruined this space. There are probably more humans living here than fae, this is why you shouldn't anchor Skyshire to Commonweald, after all it is called common for a reason."

I blink, pulling back a bit. Byron just looks amused by her statement, and I'm pretty sure that Marvin only knows that her lips moved and has no idea that she actually said anything with the blank way that he is staring at her. It's like he's never seen a fae before.

Which I know isn't the case since I am in fact a fae.

"You're so right," he murmurs after an overly long moment of strained silence.

This causes Byron to start laughing outright. Marvin blinks surprised, seeming to finally snap a little out of his daze and look over at Byron who is standing there with his hand covering his mouth trying to stifle the laugh.

"What?" he demands.

"Nothing," Byron replies with a snicker, which is very clearly a lie but since he is a human, he doesn't get called out for it.

"Come along, you three," Istaria says impatiently. "I haven't got all day for your lollygagging. The dragons are this way."

"Dragons?" I ask, tripping a bit on a slightly uneven cobblestone as I hurry after her.

"Did you think you would *walk* to the academy?" she asks, her voice dripping with condescension.

Byron glances at me an amused smile quirking the corner of his mouth, but whether he is amused at my expense,

Istaria's, or this whole situation in general, I have no idea. "We're in Skyshire now, Lo. We travel like the fae."

Ironic, a human being the one to tell the fae this.

"This is why we brought you along, Byron," Marvin says quickly with a grin pointed at me as if he is glad that Byron proved him right. I have to bite my tongue to keep from telling him to going back to mooning over Istaria. "Because I, for one, know very little about the fae."

"And here I thought you invited me because of my exceptional conversation skills... and the fact that you needed some brawn for your company."

"I was adequately equipped to get us here safely," I reply in a low tone, crossing my arms. Byron is so aggravating. Here we are in a gorgeous new city, and he wants to talk about his *brawn*? He's the grandson of a blacksmith, indeed he has spent the past several years taking over his grandfather's duties as the village blacksmith, of course he is strong. There's no need to rub it in, however... or even bring it up.

Byron chuckles. I narrow my eyes, but whatever he finds funny he seems to decide not to elaborate. "Well, my family, for better or for worse have had dealings with the fae."

"My family has had dealings with the fae, too," I mutter.

"Ha!" Byron stops walking and plants his hands on his hips as he laughs. "That's hilarious." He reaches up wiping a tear from his eye and then looks up to see that Istaria is halfway down the street and seems to not care if she leaves us behind. He picks up his pace, grinning at me as he goes. "I never struck you for being so funny. You were always too moody."

I snap my mouth shut and glower at him which probably only proves his point but what am I supposed to say? That I'm only moody around him because I hate his whole existence? I wait for Marvin to pipe up and tell Byron that I'm plenty pleasant and amusing when in the right company, but he never does.

"But as I was saying, from what my ma said from her experiences traveling Skyshire, people had to ride a dragon or some other form of flying beast to get between cities in Skyshire."

"Like a Pegasus," I breathe as I look up in time to see a magnificent white steed fly overhead, its feathered wings catching the sunlight as it goes.

"A Pegasus does fly so it would count," Byron replies in a patronizing tone. He glances up at that moment and his hand snakes forward, resting on my lower back as he quickens his pace.

"What are you doing?" I hiss, shrinking away.

"The road gets more congested ahead, we need to catch up if we don't want to lose Istaria in the crowd." He pulls his gaze from the road ahead to smirk at me. "The hand was to determine that I don't lose you either."

"I wouldn't mind losing you," I mutter.

"Hey, what about me?" Marvin demands from behind. He is puffing as he picks up his pace to keep up with us as we struggle to keep up with Istaria who is walking through the center of this Skyshire city like she is floating on a little cloud. She is moving so gracefully that I don't even see her head bob up and down. Her hair sways though.

I'm not sure which is more unsettling. Her way of walking or that spell on her.

Byron holds his hand out to him. "Sure, I'll hold your hand as well." He narrows his eyes at me before turning up his nose in fake contempt. At least, I assume it is fake given his sudden shift in mood, although why anyone would fake that emotion, I have no idea. "After all it's just a friendly gesture."

"I'll friendly gesture you off this floating rock if you touch me again."

"That doesn't even make any sense," Marvin says finally catching up to us. I notice that he doesn't accept Byron's proffered hand despite having asked for it. I smirk as we turn and start down the street again, leaving Byron empty handed.

He may have won the heart of every other girl in Woodsbury Grove, but he won't have me. I can see through his boyish antics for what they are. Annoying. Immature. Abhorrent.

Now that we are walking more quickly, we start to catch up to Istaria and her strange ghostly walk, despite the extra foot traffic in the streets. The streets themselves wind around buildings and through stalls where vendors try to sell their wares just like any other town. In some places, there are patches of grass growing in triangular sections of land behind stalls or between houses, blocked off from the street by a small wall so that you would have to step over it to trod upon the grass. The occasional tree even shoots up, certainly not as numerous as they were in the woods or around Woodsbury Grove, but trees all the same. Tall, majestic trees whose branches scrape the roofs of the stone buildings.

Here in the center of the city with no view of the edge one could almost forget that they hung suspended in the sky.

I honestly don't know what to feel now that I'm here in Skyshire, but I do know that I feel something. Perhaps, it is a little bit of awe, mixed in with a fear of falling... or maybe I'm just getting peckish. After all, we have been traveling all day, fought off cultists, were nearly eaten by living vines, and I have yet to have my supper.

Everyone here seems so caught up in their own activities. I see a woman buying bread with some form of pink sparkles on it from a vendor while trying to keep a hand clamped on her pointed eared child. Two men are standing off to the side in the shade of an oak tree talking. Other people rush to and fro. No one has time for the strangers in their city. No one even notices us.

I suppose that makes sense. With how many strangers they likely have pass through their port city. Still, it makes me feel a little lonely. I try to catch the pointy eared boy's eyes and smile at him, but he ducks behind his mother's skirts. I pull my eyes away and focus on walking.

The sun has begun setting by the time we make it through to the other side of the city. Purple and pink hues streak the sky, staining the clouds and when I look up, I can begin to make out the first stars, shyly peeking out. Their twinkle is barely visible, looking more like a faint dust sprinkled across the sky. The temperature has begun to drop with the sun and now a cool wind blows across us, replacing the sweltering heat of earlier today.

The buildings immediately stop, replaced by an open area filled with round flat stone circles. They stretch on across the space, sometimes overlapping, some stone areas higher than the rest. To the right, I can make out a massive structure. It looks like stalls, like what Marvin's father would have on his farm to house his horses, only it is much larger. To the left the world just simply ends, it drops off to sun-streaked sky and the dark form of what must be trees below us.

I swallow feeling a little squeamish. If that's the top of trees so far below us... then I don't want to think about it.

"This is the landing field and stables," Istaria says. She's come to a stop just in front of us. She turns, her nose scrunching when her hair whips in her face. "This is where people who travel through Skyshire keep their beasts or those that wish to travel to Skyshire must rent some."

"So, if you came from Skyshire and you were heading straight to another part of Skyshire... why did you feel the need to pass through Commonweald?" I ask, reaching up to tuck a portion of my hair behind my ear so that it will stop whipping in my face. Although it's not nearly as bad as Istaria's hair so I suppose I shouldn't complain. "Wouldn't that put you *out* of your way?"

"I uh... I had to go to Commonweald on some business," she says. It's getting rather dim, but it seems as if her cheeks are colored slightly.

"Huh," I mutter. It seems odd that a pureblooded high fae would have business in Commonweald, the land of the filthy humans... or so they would call them. But despite Istaria's lacking explanation, I don't see why she would lie about something so small.

If a fae is caught in the act of a lie they must pay recompense to the person they lied to. In some cases, they have been forbidden from ever lying again. This is not a threat that my people take lightly.

If we lie, we lie carefully so that we will not get caught.

Well, I speak of other fae here. The ones who have to resort to cunning to get ahead. I'd much rather focus on my own merit, work hard for what I want. Perhaps that makes me like a human, but then the humans raised me when the fae wouldn't have me, so it makes sense that I would pick up on their ways.

A figure striding toward us catches my attention. He's a tall fae with straight shoulders and hair as white as the clouds.

He doesn't greet us at all, just looks us over with a keen eye. "I'm the stablemaster," is all he says.

"We need transport to the Gilded Academy," Istaria says, smoothing a hand over her skirts which lift back up, whipping through the air.

The fae grunts his eyes flicking over her. "What's wrong with you?"

It's the first real acknowledgement of her condition. I think we're kind of trying to ignore it, but this fae's statement makes it difficult to do so.

"I would rather not talk about it," she says her voice going a little high like she might descend into hysterics if he pushes the issue.

He shrugs, his eyes flicking over the rest of us. "Just the four of you, then?"

She nods. "Indeed."

"Demetrius!" he hollers and a boy a year or two younger than me pops out of almost nowhere. He must have been under one of the elevated platforms.

"Yes, sir?"

"Saddle up two dragons for our visitors here."

The boy bobs his head before turning and racing off toward the stables.

"Only two dragons?" I ask with a frown. I hope he doesn't expect us to all ride on only two dragons.

He rolls his eyes. "You won't be riding on their *backs*. They will pull the carriage."

"Oh," I mutter, quietly.

"Imagine how amazing it would be to ride a dragon though," Byron says, his eyes on the massive beasts that the stable boy has begun leading out of the stable. Their wings trail along on the ground behind them as they shuffle forward onto one of the large platforms.

"Keep imagining," the stablemaster says gruffly. "I'm not going to risk your family coming after me and demanding recompense if you happen to fall off my beasts."

"A pity," Byron breathes.

"Not really," Marvin says with a nervous chuckle. "I'd rather not have to watch you fall to your death. That would be traumatizing."

Byron starts toward the dragons, following the stablemaster who turned and started walking away without a word. "Why are you assuming that I'd fall off the dragon?"

"Because you are you."

Byron turns to him, arching a single brow. "What is that supposed to mean?"

Marvin shrugs. "You're a chronic showoff."

Which is probably the meanest thing you'll ever hear Marvin say. Also, probably the truest.

Byron turns so that he is walking backwards. "Willow, tell him that I'm not a showoff." Just as the words are out of his mouth, his foot lands on the edge of one of the platforms and he begins to fall backwards. Quick as a flash, my hand shoots out and grabs him by the front of his shirt, and then I yank him toward me.

Byron's eyes are wide as he stares down at me, breathing hard. "Uh, thanks?" he says when he has a second for his brain to catch up with what happened. Unfortunately, my brain is still floundering.

My eyes flick down to my hand still wrapped around the material of his shirt.

Did I just *help* Byron Coalbiter?

I yank my hand back like the touch of his shirt burned me.

I'm not entirely sure what was running through my mind or why I didn't let him fall and twist his ankle, but I blame my reflexes. I pull back, flexing my hand as I stare at the creases that it left on his shirt. I stride past him, pursing my lips. "I shouldn't lie," I say at last. "It could end poorly for me."

I don't dare risk a second glance back at Byron as I race forward. I come to a stop beside the dragons a feeling of awe replacing the one of muddled confusion that I felt. The beasts are majestic, far larger than anything that I had imagined. They tower above us, larger than the tallest building I have ever seen. Massive horns grace its head and smoke curls from its narrow snout. The scales are so large they're about the size of dinner plates and they look almost sharp to the touch. Chains that are about as thick as my arm wrap around the two dragon's necks attaching them to a carriage.

"These are red dragons," Marvin says, coming to a stop next to me. "They are the largest dragons capable of being domesticated. Despite their massive size, they're actually normally quite docile."

I turn to him, nudging his arm. "Do I want to know how you know that?"

"I make it my business to know my dragons," he says with a sniff, before reaching into his satchel and pulling out a book with a cracked binding. It looks like it has been well read. The words *An Encyclopedia of Dragons* is printed across the binding.

I huff a small laugh and shake my head. "Marvin, remind me not to be seen in public with you."

"I hope your wild fae sensibilities are not bothered at seeing an imprisoned animal," Istaria says, stepping up between me and Marvin.

I look over my shoulder half expecting to see another fae has joined us, but the only person on that side of me is Byron. And he's as human as the day is long. I whip my gaze back to Istaria, feeling my eyes widen when I see her looking directly at me.

"Are you talking to me?" I ask, surprised by how high my voice comes out. "I'm no wild fae. You had it right the first time, I'm low-magic."

My problem is that my magic is nearly nonexistent, not that my magic is uncontrollable.

"Hmmm," she says not looking convinced. "I've changed my mind. You look wild to me."

I pull back, blinking repeatedly. I do? Last I checked, I wasn't running around barefoot wearing antlers with leaves sticking out of my hair.

"Wait!" I call as Istaria starts toward the carriage. One of the dragons snorts at my outburst and twitches its tail. I wince holding up my hands to pacify the creature and take off toward Istaria who hasn't stopped walking. "What do you mean that I look like a wild fae?" I demand, coming to a stop next to her.

I'd always thought that I just looked like a fae. Fae like humans are capable of bearing many varying appearances. I didn't realize that there was a specific *look* of the wild fae. But then, I've also never met a wild fae. They usually stick to themselves, and their cities made of trees, refusing to associate with humans and definitely not associating with other fae.

She pauses, her foot already in the carriage, her eyes flicking up and down my form before she arches an eyebrow.

"Well, for one your coloring is too earthy, your eyes green, your hair that reddish brown." She waves her hand, her nose wrinkling. "You have a, well, a wild look about you."

Says the girl with a spell of wind whipping through her hair, leaving it so tangled that a week's worth of brushing probably won't get rid of it.

She finishes ducking into the carriage without another word or explanation. I ball my hand into a fist my mind racing. It's true that I never knew my parents, but I couldn't be wild. Little as my magic is, it's controllable. I've never had any issues summoning light or controlling its brightness. Control was never the issue; it was just the sheer inadequacy of my magic that always made me ashamed.

All of a sudden, a hand is brushing against my knuckles. I blink, turning to find myself staring into Byron's sparkling blue eyes. "Don't take her words to heart. Istaria is used to seeing high fae, she has no idea that regular fae are out there and she's just trying to explain away what she doesn't understand. Besides, you don't look very wild to me." Byron's eyes flick over me, the corner of his mouth turning up. "You're still the same old, Lo, as ever."

Somehow, Byron's words only work to make me feel worse.

CHAPTER ELEVEN

The silence in the carriage is palpable. Somehow, I wound up sitting next to Istaria. Not that there were a lot of options. I'm also forced to be across from Byron and my knee bumps his as the dragons start forward with a shuddering takeoff. The carriage rolls forward and as it does, I start to realize just how crazy this is. Because now we are in a carriage being pulled by dragons who are being controlled by a fae we've never even met before today, and we are rolling right toward the edge of this city... and the steep drop to Commonweald below.

I can see the edge of this island of Skyshire quickly approaching through the window. I suck in a deep breath, beginning to feel panic well up within me. I'm considering diving out the window and saving myself when we suddenly run out of ground. The carriage drops slightly, but then I see the dragons spread out their wings, their impressive wingspan blocking out much of the view beyond the window and somehow the carriage doesn't drop like a weight.

It must be some sort of fae engineering or magic that I'm too human-raised to understand, but either way I'm grateful to not be plummeting to the ground. I exhale loudly, feeling myself relax as I do something shifts under my hand. I glance out of the corner of my eye to see that in my moment of panic I had reached out and grasped Byron. No, worse than that, I had clamped my hand around his knee.

"You're going to be all right," Byron says. "Do you really think I'd let us all plummet to our deaths?"

Byron Coalbiter may have some fancy magic for a black-smith's grandson, but not even he can defy gravity, so I'm not entirely sure why he thinks his words would be reassuring.

I blush and yank my hand back, shaking it out before I settle for wiping it on my pants to try to get rid of the feel of Byron. "Sorry about that."

"Hey, no worries. You can squeeze my knee anytime you want to."

I glower at him pausing in wiping my hand down my leg. "And what about punching you in the nose? How often can I do that?"

"As little as possible." Byron gestures up at his straight nose. "I prefer to look pretty. You wouldn't believe how often it gets me out of trouble."

I roll my eyes and he grins, his eyes twinkling. "I'm just teasing. You know I'm not like that. My grandfather certainly didn't raise someone who would make a habit out of getting in trouble."

"I always got too nervous when I did something wrong, I'd turn myself in," Marvin says.

I shift in my seat. "I never had anyone to sin against." As soon as the words are out of my mouth I realize that they aren't true. Perhaps I never worried about sinning against an absent god like the Maker, but I do have the good people of Woodsbury. They took me in, and I've always tried to do right by them. I'd always clean and help with other chores for the families that took me in during the time that I was staying with them. I did my best not to seem like a burden or a strain on them financially, even if that was how I still always felt inside.

"Why are we talking of sinning?" Istaria demands, coldly. She straightens her shoulders and lifts her nose. "I certainly have strange companions."

I won't argue with her there. I suppose we are strange, the three of us. All from our tiny village and on our way to try to join the most esteemed knightly order there is.

After all paladins are known for the sacrifices they make to join the order and serve their Maker, templars are known for their mystery, wardens for their close ties to nature, mercenaries for their corruption, but the knight champions? They are known for their distinction.

To be chosen by a high fae to be their personal protector, the extension of their arm in a sense... well that is an honor above all else and one that is not lightly given. To become gilded, you must be chosen, and I intend to be chosen by Menavillion.

My stomach flops as I glance at Byron. That is if I can convince the fae lord to turn his back on *this* protégé who wields his magic.

I wish I could spend this carriage ride in anticipation or even just admiring the view. Commonweald is hard to make out below in the darkness now that the sun has set, but the stars are brilliant and so close. It makes me wonder why not everyone chooses to live in the sky.

But deep down I mostly just stew and fret and wonder if this dream of mine will be stolen from me. No... not just stolen. Snatched away by Byron Coalbiter. Now there is a boy born with everything. He has a wonderful grandfather who loves him, an esteemed position in our village, powerful magic, and an easy way with people.

Why does he need Menavillion's patronage? Why can't he just be a blacksmith for the village that always loved him and leave me alone as I try to finally find some place in this world to call my own. Somewhere that I will not have to live off the charity of others just to get by.

I can't tell if the journey is long or short, it somehow feels both. I'm surprised when I feel the carriage jolt and yet my stiff legs tell me that I have been riding in the carriage for more than enough time to make them cramp up.

At the second jolt, I manage to tense my leg and brace myself enough that I don't wind up flying forward and landing in Byron's lap. Forget the knee squeezing episode, if I wound up in his lap that is something I would never be able to live down.

The carriage lurches again and it takes every amount of strength in my core to keep from flying forward. Istaria sits up higher, not seemingly phased by our jolting carriage. "We're here."

"The academy," Byron breathes.

Marvin is starting to look a little green. "What was my father thinking sending me here?"

I reach across Istaria and clasp his hand. "We're in this together. We'll get through this."

I startle slightly when Byron puts his hand over mine. I glance at him out of the corner of my eye, but he's focused

121

on Marvin. "We'll put Woodsbury on the map, the three of us."

Barely waiting for the carriage to still, Istaria steps out without a single "by your leave" and I scurry to follow her. I will be there when she meets with Menavillion to make absolutely certain that she doesn't leave me out in her recounting of her heroic rescue. I need to make a good impression on him, and despite her strange views on me, like seeing me as a wild fae, I did save Istaria's life. That has to count for something, right? And sure, Byron was there to help save her as well, but I'm the one who actually entered that chamber and cut her free.

My boot lands on hard stone, and I glance around. Behind the carriage, I can see the dark form of a platform just end... nothing but empty air waits beyond. There is a warm glow on the other side of the dragons, as I step around them, I take it in for the first time.

The Academy of the Gilded Knight.

Nothing about this moment is exactly how I imagined it. For one, it's too dark to take in much of the view from up here. Torches line the academy's walls, throwing a glow around us, but casting all else in shadow. Secondly, I'm standing next to two massive dragons whose majesty make the academy pale in comparison. Thirdly, I'm much colder than I ever imagined I would be.

But the academy itself... now *that* is exactly how I expected.

A stone structure that is so large I wouldn't be able to see around it even if it weren't a dark night. Two long windows have firelight reflect off their glass as they rise up over an equally large door that is so big that I think maybe one of the red dragons could fit through it. A white flag with a golden unicorn on it snaps in the wind, the emblem of the Gilded Academy, most champions take on their patron's insignia, but some also find a way to incorporate this unicorn in their armor.

The sound of roaring water meets my ears. It's too dark to see the source, but I've heard of rivers in Skyshire that spill out over the edge and fall down to lakes that have formed below in Commonweald.

A young man steps out through a crack in the large doors and scurries to Istaria's side. She whispers a command to him, probably demanding that he summon her betrothed, meanwhile Marvin appears to be paying the stablemaster for the ride.

I hear a low whistle beside me and glance over my shoulder to see that Byron is now standing there. "It's a sight, isn't it?"

"I would have used the term *magnificent, grandiose, impressive*... but I suppose you're right. It's a *sight*."

He grins and nudges my arm. "I can hardly believe that I made it this far. I always intended to attend this academy, but I guess I never actually thought I'd get here. Just like a child dreaming of growing up, the inevitable future always seems so far away until you're living in it."

I turn to him, my mouth gaping open. "You've dreamed of attending this academy since you were a child?"

"And you think I rolled out of bed one morning and decided to be a fae's knight champion?" Byron lifts his hand and waves his arm out. "This is the culmination of a lifetime of hopes and dreams." His mouth twists slightly. "Maybe not mine, but somebody's, and now I'm here."

He shivers, but I don't think it has anything to do with the cool night air which picks up as the dragons take off again, leaving us here. "Can't believe that I'm actually here," he says, more softly this time.

"Yeah, me neither," I say. I blink, trying to make out his expression in the flickering torchlight and the shine of the stars. "What do you mean—"

"It's really too bad that I won't be able to stay here longer," he continues not seeming to have heard me, "but I need to be on the fast track for knighthood for my grandfather's sake."

Byron's words cause my stomach to sink like a stone as I'm reminded that despite the fact that we share a dream,

Byron is a problem. He wants what I want, and I can't let him have it if I am to attain my own childhood hopes. I grapple trying to find something to say that might make that clear to Byron. That we aren't friends, we can never be friends, even if I wanted us to be.

Which I don't, of course.

Do I?

Just then there is a loud creak as the door is pushed wide open and in strides a tall fae with shining golden hair. The color is so bright that it seems to almost glow in the darkness. He is wearing a draping robe that flows down around him and a crown that appears to have been made out of the stars themselves. His eyes, however, are dark as the night as they look over us, briefly forming a judgement in a single second before they turn to Istaria.

A half smile forms on his lips but then it disappears. "Istaria, my betrothed, what has become of you?"

My pulse quickens. Lord Menavillion.

"Cultists," she says, her eyes ever so briefly turning to a knight standing to the right of Menavillion. I startle a little when I see him, I had been so focused on the high fae that I hadn't noticed that he wasn't alone. The knight is decked in a suit of armor made all of gold, the visor of his helmet is closed concealing his identity, but who he is, is already clear to all. He's a knight champion in service of

Lord Menavillion. This silent figure in full armor is exactly what I hope to someday become.

I will admit, I imagined it to be a slightly more glamorous lifestyle. Not that I would become a person who some people might even miss entering a room.

Perhaps Byron is thinking the same thing because he is staring at the knight with a somewhat hurt and twisted look on his face.

Istaria continues, her tone completely even. "I was kidnapped by them; they must have cast a dark spell over me. I stand before you now only due to the kindness of these strangers."

"You seem very calm, My Pearl, considering the atrocities that have been committed against you."

"Would you rather I be a sobbing puddle at your feet?"

My eyes dart between both the fae as they stare each other down, neither of their faces showing a hint of emotion. I frown, wondering what their problems are. Are they incapable of showing that they care? Of embracing their future spouse? Is this what it's like to actually be a fae?

If it is, then I don't want it.

Menavillion finally breaks his gaze away from Istaria and turns back to us. "And these are the people I have to thank for your safe return?"

"My debts are my own, but your appreciation is free to be given." Istaria folds her hands in front of her.

I step forward, opening my mouth. I'm shaking all over, but I'm not about to risk my chance to introduce myself to Menavillion. His eyes skip right over me and lock on Byron. "You're a Coalbiter," he murmurs. "You carry your family resemblance well."

Byron dips his head. "I'm honored you would recognize me, My Lord."

The knight behind Menavillion shifts and clears his throat slightly. I agree, the obeisance is a bit unsettling, but maybe that's because he beat me to it. I ball my hand into a fist, working to steady my nerves.

"My name is Willow," I squeak. I pause and clear my throat. I dip my chin as Menavillion turns back to me. "It's an honor to meet you, My Lord."

I wince I realize that it's too close to what Byron said.

Menavillion raises a single brow. "Are you a fae girl?"

"She's a wild fae," Istaria says, "Can you not tell by looking at her?"

"Hmm," is all Menavillion says.

"I'm not—"

"And who is this?" he asks gesturing to Marvin.

"I honestly don't remember," Istaria says. Marvin's head droops.

127

"This is Marvin," Byron says, stepping forward and slapping Marvin on the shoulder. "Without him, we never would have made it here, he's the one who paid our passage."

"I see, well I am *charmed.* "Menavillion nods his head. "I hope that you do not mind, but I am a busy man. I thank you for the service that you paid to my betrothed." His eyes linger on Byron, causing my heart to pick up its rate. "I look forward to seeing what you have to offer here at this academy, Coalbiter. It will be interesting to have another of you in my company."

My stomach drops like I swallowed a stone. Then Menavillion turns and walks away as if he doesn't carry my future hopes and dreams with him.

CHAPTER TWELVE

A fter Menavillion leaves, an academy porter comes to show us to our rooms. Since they arrived at the same time, Byron and Marvin get to share their room. I'm kind of jealous of them, to be able to share a room with someone they know.

I'll be having to bunk with a stranger. Not that I'm not used to it. Although I suppose I couldn't necessarily call anyone at Woodsbury Grove a stranger, but some could certainly classify as strange.

I inhale deeply, staring down the door, trying to calm my nerves. They've only grown since I said goodnight to Byron and Marvin. I feel so much more alone with them now in their rooms. Not that I'm allowing myself to feel comforted by Byron's presence here at the academy with me—not with all the troubles it brings me. Still, I wish that Marvin was here. He would make me feel better.

I raise my hand to knock, but then I realize that it's my room and it's late.

I'd probably disturb my roommate more by knocking rather than sneaking in. I push the door open, slipping through. Someone exhales and turns over in one of the two beds in the room. I make my way through the dark, dropping my satchel down and collapsing into the other bed, not bothering to change.

Almost immediately as I close my eyes, sleep claims me.

My next conscious thought is to register how bright it is. I groan, and roll over but the brightness finds me in the crevice of the bed I tried to find sanctuary in. I force my eyes open as a jolt shoots through me when I realize that brightness is sunlight. I sit up with a gasp glancing around wide-eyed as I try to figure out how late it is.

My eyes land on a girl with golden hair standing near the bed. She is already up and dressed in padded armor, her arms raised as she pulls her luxurious locks into a braid.

She pauses in braiding her hair and glances at me. "You must be my new roommate. My name is Chastmire."

"Willow," I reply reaching up and rubbing my eyes. "What time is it?"

"Time for me to be leaving." She nods her head to me. "Sorry, Willow, but I'm not here to make friendships. I want to be a champion, and I'm not letting anything distract me from that. Stay out of my way, don't try to keep me up at night, and we should get along just fine."

"I..." I stutter as she finishes tying the ribbon and strides off.

However, she pauses at the door and offers me a tight smile. "Sorry if I'm coming off strong, but there's not a chance in Skyshire that I'm going back home without that title. I'm not here for friendships, or to make bonds... I'm here to become a knight and that's it."

"You..." I continue sputtering.

"It was nice to meet you, Willow," she says before she opens the door and strides off, leaving me sitting in my bed completely overwhelmed and a little bit confused as to what I'm supposed to do next. I arrived so late last night that I didn't get the chance to figure out how things are run here. I have no idea when fast is broken and what sort of academic studies will be expected of me here. I assume there is someone I can speak to get all of this information, but I don't know where to even find them.

Suddenly, the world seems so big and the future so uncertain. I don't think the reality of me leaving Woodsbury quite sunk in until this moment but suddenly I feel as if my stomach is doing dozens of cartwheels. I want to rush out of this room and find Byron and Marvin... *no*.

I shake my head. I want to find Marvin and Marvin alone. Just because Byron is from home doesn't mean that I can find comfort in him. Out of all the strangers in this new academy, the boy from my hometown is still my biggest threat.

I cannot allow this bout of homesickness to blind me to that fact.

I push to my feet but freeze when I look down at myself. My pants are torn and muddied and there appears to be a little bit of blood on it. I swallow hard with a grimace. This was my best outfit, I wore it in the hopes of making a good impression at my new home, not thinking that I would wind up rescuing a damsel in distress and flee through the woods and battle evil vines.

A knock sounds on my door, I whip my head around just as it opens and Istaria strides through. I don't know which is stranger, the fact that she is carrying a heaping pile of fabrics or that her hair and dress are still being whipped around her like she is caught in the middle of a storm that only she can feel.

"Istaria," I say, my voice coming out strained with surprise. "What are you doing here? Are you still cursed?"

"I'm here because I owe you a favor, believe me, I'm not just paying some social call. And, yes, I'm cursed still because my lordly betrothed has not figured out what is wrong with me yet."

I reach up, gesturing around my head, lifting up a strand of hair. "Is that annoying?"

"Exceedingly, much like having to spend time with you. So, let's make this quick so that I may be able to leave this whole affair behind me." She steps forward, thrusting the fabric in her hands out until it is colliding with my chest. I scramble to catch it as she drops it.

"What's all this?"

Istaria exhales as she narrows her eyes at me. She gestures to the pile now in my arms. "This is my repayment for you saving my life. Now I owe you nothing."

I lift the top item off, my mouth dropping open when I realize that it is a blue shirt made of the finest, most shimmery material I've ever seen. I turn wide-eyes to Istaria. "Did the boys get gifts too?"

"They asked for favors from me." Istaria's mouth purses. "Marvin asked for a kiss."

"And Byron?"

"He wanted an audience with Menavillion?" She lifts a single shoulder as if she couldn't care less despite the fact that her words send my knees trembling. "Byron mentioned that you might want some new clothes. Something about you not having many outfits and ruined what you had while rescuing me... or something equally plebian." She gestures to the pile. "Many of these were my old clothes that had been sent ahead of me, but I managed to find some wild fae clothing as well for you."

"Wild fae? You shouldn't have," I mutter dryly.

The smile that she gives me is almost cruel. "Wouldn't want you being homesick, after all."

"I'm not—" I begin, but Istaria turns away and strides off not bothering to argue her case. I snap my mouth shut, deciding that the fact that this high lady seems to think that I'm a wild fae is the least of my problems.

Because in return for saving Istaria, Byron got a private audience with Menavillion.

And all I got is an armful of clothes.

CHAPTER THIRTEEN

A s I step out of my room something flits in my face. I pull back, opening my eyes just in time to see a pixie whiz down the hall. About the size of a dragonfly and with skin and hair of gold, pixies tend to stick around fae, drawn in by their magic.

Which means that I didn't see any pixies in human populated Woodsbury Grove. I shake my head, wondering how many collisions I'll have with pixies now that I'm here in Skyshire. I step forward, but something rustles under my foot. I glance down to see a bit of parchment sticking out from underneath the edge of my boot. I bend over, picking it up, squinting at the blank surface. Just as I'm about to crumple it up I notice a dark line. Slowly as if someone is writing on the paper while I'm holding it, letters appear.

Welcome to the Academy of the Gilded Knight, Willow Brightbringer...

I nearly drop the note, wondering how it knows my name, but then I realize that the note likely is enchanted to address whoever is holding it. After all, this note is literally writing itself and I'm concerned about it knowing who I am?

This isn't Commonweald anymore, I'm in the land of the fae, a place of magic. One that I don't necessarily belong in yet... but perhaps I will someday.

The note goes on to highlight the times and locations of the requisite classes. Battle training, strategies, histories, and of course fae etiquette. Everything that will make a person desirable to be chosen as a champion and everything a knight needs to make it through the world.

It seems as if the main events, however, will be a series of feasts with each of the fae lords who are here in the hopes of gaining a knight. These dinners are important because it will help the high fae discover who we are and what we may have to offer.

Students are encouraged to attend as many feasts as they would like, but my eyes are only on the time of Menavillion's feast which appears to be in about a week.

It also appears that there will be several mock battles held throughout the semester so that we knights to be may be able to show off our prowess.

There appears that there will be many mock battles and feasts throughout the year, but the first two are important because they will create our first impression. Not to mention that some high fae probably don't want to stay here and watch knights be trained all year.

The most promising will be snatched up early. I know that it's Byron's intention to be one of the early chosen, and while I wouldn't mind spending more time at this academy, learning what I can, if I want to beat him then I have to be better than him and to be chosen before him.

The note ends with a message that in order to find my way to any place I have only to ask the academy, and it will send whisps to guide me. I have no idea what that is supposed to mean, but a signature by *Headmaster Rogelus* shows up on the bottom of the page and suddenly the whole message disappears save for the class schedule.

I blink and turn the paper over, but no scrawling script appears on that side. It appears that I am now on my own to figure this all out.

I fold the paper, placing it into the pocket of a pair of pants that Istaria had given me, they are black and sleek and pair well with the beautiful blue shirt that had caught my eye earlier and a black vest that I have on over it.

I took some time to do my hair in more than just a sloppy braid and I'll admit, I'm actually feeling pretty confident. At least I was feeling confident until I started wondering if I'm expected to speak to an empty hallway.

"Uh... can you show me where to break my fast?" I ask, my voice coming out in a hesitant whisper. As soon as the words leave my mouth a path of pale white smoke appears in front of me. I stumble back a step in surprise. The mist doesn't shift with my movement and after I've caught myself, I reach my foot out and touch it to the mist. It draws back as soon as I come in contact with it. The majority of the trail remains ahead, twisting down the hallway, but disappearing where I step.

I start after the smoke, making my way through the grand stone hall of the academy until I reach a pair of thick double doors. I push one open a crack, grimacing as I find it slightly heavier than I anticipated. Still, I manage to get it wide enough to slip through. As I do so, the mist disappears and I find myself in a hub of activity.

Plates clatter against tables and chairs scrape on the stone floors, chatter fills the air. I glance around, taking in three long tables full of students. Still more tables covered in food line the walls.

This must be the banquet hall. My initial impression is to feel utterly overwhelmed. There are so many people here, far more than I expected, but then I feel chagrin. To be a fae's champion is an esteemed position, why would I expect people not to vie for this position? After all, if some homeless fae from Woodsbury could find her way to this academy, then surely others have journeyed from all across Commonweald, indeed even Skyshire, for this opportunity.

I duck my head, hurriedly grabbing a plate and stuffing it full of food that I barely even register. I think it is mostly scones and treats and a few bits of fruit before I hurry to the nearest seat and plunk down. As I do so I realize that the mist is nowhere to be seen. I lift my foot glancing down.

"If you're looking for the mist it disappears after you reach your destination." I startle at the voice, nearly knocking my plate off the table with my elbow. I whip my head around to take in the girl I had apparently sat next to here at the end of the table. She's a fae with traditional markings painted on her face, swirls across her chin and around her sparkling blue eyes. Her hair is pulled back to reveal her pointed ears. It's still strange to see fae wherever I look, after being the only fae in Woodsbury Grove, I've grown accustomed to thinking of myself as the outlier.

The corner of her mouth hitches up into an amused smile. "And if you're wondering why you don't see a bunch of crossing paths of mist from the other students, that's because the pathway is only visible to the person that asks for it." Her mouth twists. "So, you don't have to be worried about the hallways always being full of mist or not being able to find your path because it intersects with someone else's."

"Well... thank you for that information."

She grunts as she takes a bite of a particularly juicy piece of fruit, droplets fly onto the table. I stare down at them. She licks her fingers loudly. "Oh, you're welcome. You're new, right? I haven't seen your face here before and I'm particularly good at faces."

I nod smiling at her. "My name is Willow, I arrived just last night."

"Pepper," she says scrunching her nose as she smiles. "Speaking of faces... that one is also new and particularly handsome."

I turn following her gaze, although I think I already knew who it was she was talking about. Sure, enough there at the next table over, sitting in the midst of a large group of admirers that he somehow managed to gather in the short time he has been here is Byron Coalbiter.

"Typical," I mutter.

"Hmm, what was that?" Pepper asks, not taking her eyes off Byron.

I stretch my fingers underneath the table, I straighten when I see a girl laugh and fall into Byron's lap. He seems to snort while trying to drink and a chorus of laughter fills the room. I spot Marvin on his other side, but he doesn't seem to even notice the other people there, he is just focused on eating. Which is also true to his character. "Nothing, just wondering why I'm surprised is all."

At just that moment, Byron looks up. He nudges Marvin who also looks up and then scootches to the side making a space for me, well assuming one of the girls hanging off him doesn't fall into it first. Byron waves his hand as if his intentions weren't obvious enough.

"Is he waving one of us over?" Pepper breathes.

I groan, reaching up to rub at my forehead.

"Willow!" Byron shouts. "Come sit with us."

"Isn't that what you said your name was?"

I press my eyes shut, before managing a stiff nod. "Yes, uh, Byron and I grew up in the same village."

"Ahhh," she breathes. "I see."

I may be paranoid, but I don't think that she gets it at all.

Pepper rests her chin in her hand as she stares at him dreamily. "If he was from my village, I'd follow him too. Even to an academy in the sky."

"I didn't follow him," I splutter. "He followed me." I shake my head at the wide-eyed look she gives. "That is, we were supposed to travel separately, and somehow, he finagled his way into making the trip *with* me."

Her eyebrows rise as she looks me over, an impressed look on her face. "If he is your man then you better go stake your claim. The girls here seem to think that he is available."

"He's not *my* anything," I growl out. I go to shove my chair back, forgetting briefly that I'm sitting on a long bench alongside perhaps half a dozen potential knight champions. The chair doesn't budge, and it probably just ends with me looking stupid. I groan and slide out, narrowing my eyes at the bewildered look that Bryon is giving me. I grab a roll since I'm still hungry even if I'm mad and turn, stalking out of the banquet hall.

CHAPTER FOURTEEN

T he first sign of trouble is the pounding of feet behind me. I'm following the mist through the academy; I had asked it to bring me to the library so I could have
a hopefully quiet place to gather my thoughts and figure
out why I'm shaking right now.

I rip a bite out of my roll and glance over my shoulder,
groaning when I see that it's Byron chasing after me. And
here I was hoping it was someone racing to collect the
books they left somewhere.

"Hey, Lo, wait up!"

My foot stalls and I throw him the most irritated look I
can conjure. "It's *Willow*, Byron. I haven't gone by Lo for
years."

"Sorry," he says shooting me a lopsided grin. "I guess old
habits die hard."

I huff a loud sigh in return.

He glances at me out of the corner of his eye as he falls into step beside me, easily keeping up with the fast pace that I'm already setting. "Are you all right?"

"What do you mean?"

"You just looked upset when you left the banquet hall. Marvin said that you probably just needed to cool off, but I was worried especially after the very trying day we had yesterday. I wanted to make sure you were okay after all that. I mean... someone did die."

I pinch the end of my vest, rubbing my thumb across the bottom of my vest. "Marvin does know me well; I usually need to cool off on my own."

"But?" Byron prompts.

"No buts," I reply with a shake of my head. "My friend knows me well that is all."

"So, you *are* upset?" Byron prods, not seeming to take the hint that I want some space. But then, he did just follow me as I hurriedly raced off. I doubt he will catch any hints I drop when he ignored that sign of me wanting to be left alone. "Do you want to talk about it?"

Does he really think I would be acting this evasive if I wanted to talk about it?

I purse my lips. I'm about to tell him to take a hike, preferably off the edge of the academy, but what pops out instead is, "So, have you decided on your next dalliance? It seems you have a lot of potential volunteers to be your arm warmer."

Byron barks a laugh. "Wait, so this is all because you are *jealous*?"

I feel my cheeks color, although I can only assume that it is because of rage. Fortunately, the mist disappears behind a door that likely leads into the library, I shrug it open ducking inside looking for an escape.

My sanctuary is short lived since Byron follows me a second later.

"*Willow*, you don't have to be jealous of me. You know I was just wondering yesterday why we never courted back in Woodsbury."

I grab a book off the shelf and move over to a window seat, plopping down on it. "I am *not* having this conversation."

"And what conversation would you rather have?" he asks, crossing his arms and leaning back against the shelf.

"I'd rather read," I reply opening the book and holding it up, although I'll admit I can't focus on any of the words on the page. My ears are ringing, and Byron's words are cycling through my head. He was wondering why we never courted back in Woodsbury? As if the decision was only his to make? Did he not take into consideration that I despised him?

"Your book is upside down," Byron says after a long moment.

I slam my book shut and glare up at him. "What do you want from me?"

He lifts his shoulders slightly in a shrug. "I don't know, Lo." He holds up his hands in a pacifying gesture. "I'm sorry, *Willow*. I suppose I would settle for us clearing the air between us." He tilts his head, a lock of his parted bangs falling into his eyes. "Don't get me wrong, you're cute when you're grumpy, but I also don't like seeing you upset so I'm in a bit of a bind here."

"If you wanted to make me happy then leave this academy and never come back," I say before I can fully comprehend the words leaving my lips.

Byron steps back a puzzled frown taking over his carefree grin. "What are you talking about? Why would you want me to leave? We're in this together, isn't that what we said when we got here?"

"That's what *you* said."

"But... not you?" Confusion is written across his expression as he looks me over. "Why not?"

I pull my lip in, contemplating the prudency of my words, finally I shake my head with a little groan. "Because you're my rival, Byron. You always have been."

"*Rivals?*" he scoffs. "This is the first I'm hearing of this."

"Because you're denser than the black forest at the height of summer."

Byron's mouth drops open with an audible click. "Wait... are you being serious?"

I am unable to meet Byron's eyes.

"Hold on, I must be hearing this wrong. Are you saying that you *hate* me?" He sounds so genuinely hurt that I want to take back my words, but I also can't lie. And I think I've gone on too long not telling the truth. Byron deserves to hear how I really feel about him. I owe him that much.

"Hate is a very strong word," I say softly. I rub my palm against my pants and grimace. "But I do despise your charmed life and your easy manners. Everyone loves you and to top it all off you were born with a magic more powerful than most can dream of wielding. And there's the matter of Menavillion."

"What about Menavillion?" he snaps, his eyes spark like they have a live coal in them. It's fitting given his name, but I don't think I've ever seen him this livid. Apparently, it's inconceivable for him to imagine that someone might find his Ser Perfect charade sickening.

"What did you want to talk to him about?" I demand, his gaze looks blank. "Istaria told me about your requested favor."

"I just offered him a bargain," he says dismissively. "Why would you.... *Oh*." Byron stills, his whole body going still as realization dawns in his eyes. "You want Menavillion to be your patron too."

"He's only looking for one new champion this year. And I will be it."

He reaches up, massaging his forehead. "I can't believe this; all this time and you've seen me as your enemy?"

"Not enemy, rival. I want to be better than you not defeat you."

His shoulders slump. "I don't know, I'm feeling pretty defeated right about now. I thought we were friends."

My mouth twists slightly as I glance down at my hands folded on my lap. "Well, I'm sorry you feel that way. I don't know why you fostered thoughts of friendship with me when I never gave you any sign or indication of that being a possibility."

He shrugs, holding up his hands as he paces away. "I don't know, maybe because I don't assume people are plotting against me or secretly holding a grudge over something I can't control."

"And yet you conveniently manage to get a special audience with Menavillion before the rest of us can while I get clothes, so something tells me that you're doing just fine even with my secret grudges."

"You tore your best clothes," Byron says, his voice rising in pitch as he attempts to defend himself. "I thought you would appreciate my consideration, not resent me more." He turns away, drawing in a deep breath. "And here I was going to say that you looked nice in that outfit that Istaria clearly got for you."

"So, I only look nice when I am agreeing with you?" I demand, balling my fist.

Byron turns, narrowing his eyes. "All I know is that you're looking awfully ungrateful right now."

I suck in a deep breath, and Byron whips his head back around since apparently the bookshelf is better worth his attention than I am. "And what am I supposed to be grateful about?" I snap out. "I have nothing! Not that I'd expect you to understand how that feels. You have *no idea* what it's like to be weak and powerless. All my life I had no control, every meal that I ate relied on the kindness of strangers."

"You say that like it's a bad thing!"

"It was."

"You never went hungry, Willow," Byron says in a low tone. "My grandfather and the good people of Woodsbury made certain of that."

I glance down at my boot before pushing to my feet with a sharp shake of my head. "Like I said... this isn't something you'd ever be able to understand. I don't intend to be at anyone's mercy ever again, no matter how well-meaning they are." I stalk toward the door but stop, bracing myself on the doorframe as I stare at Byron's turned back. When I speak again it's only a low murmur. "I'm working to drag myself up from nothing and make a name for myself. I'm trying to make myself... to be—"

"To be what, Willow?" he demands, his voice is still hard and suddenly I'm filled with the crippling worry that I've made it so he will never give me that crooked smile again. That I'll never see him carefree, but instead he will only ever be this angry person I'm talking to now.

"*Worthy*," I whisper, my voice cracking slightly.

Byron flinches, but there is a tempest of emotions raging within me. And there's a tightness in my throat that is beginning to feel dangerously like tears. Before they manage to break loose, I fling open the door and race out of the library.

CHAPTER FIFTEEN

The observatory offers me the solitude that I had been hoping to find in the library, but now I'm left wondering if I actually wanted to be left alone with only my own thoughts for company. Not after hours of them tearing through me, forcing me to imagine every possible outcome of our conversation in the library.

I would go and attempt to locate Marvin, but he shares a room with Byron and at this hour I'm sure that both of them are in there, probably sleeping.

Like I should be.

I sigh, tilting back my head as I look up at the domed ceiling of the observatory, located at the very edge of the academy, the ceiling and circular walls of this room show the sky beyond as if there is no boundary standing between me and the stars. And yet when I reach my hand out, it meets cool stone instead of wispy cloud.

From here the stars seem so close, sparkling like a thousand jewels. I bet those stars aren't wondering if holding onto their dream is going to be the one thing that destroys them.

I can't get the look in Byron's face after I told him that I saw him as a rival out of my mind. I'd often imagined how smug I would feel if I finally managed to strike Byron Coalbiter low, but I don't feel smug at all.

You know I was just wondering yesterday why we never courted back in Woodsbury...

And then there is that statement. Had Byron been about to admit that he was starting to like me? I shake that thought out of my head. No, he told me that only to distract me.

Except he said it before he had any idea that I had designs on a knighthood with Menavillion.

I press my eyes shut and knock my forehead against the stone wall, when I open my eyes, I stare out at the stars only inches from my face. I feel a little like I should see my reflection the same way I would if I were viewing the stars through the pond back at home.

But no, these stars are a magical illusion of the sky, and the pond back home is miles away.

"I wish you would just show me what I truly want," I whisper to the stars that aren't even here, and even if they were they wouldn't be able to help me anyway.

As the words escape my lips, I hear a slight fizzing sound; I look over my shoulder to see a trail of white mist leading from my feet and through the door. My mouth drops open with a near audible click as I realize that the academy must have thought that I was addressing it. I'm not sure how the mist is able to lead me to what I truly want or how it can intrinsically know what I want—especially when I don't even know what I want—but I'm not about to argue with magic. Not when I'm feeling as lost as I currently am.

I step after the mist, following it and leaving the observatory behind. It weaves through the halls ahead of me, disappearing around a corner. I take off after it, running through the dark halls which are lit only by the faint glow of the white mist. I don't even know if there is a curfew at this academy, but I may very well be breaking it.

I do my best to tread lightly on the stones, while still not sacrificing speed as I race to follow the white mist winding ahead of me. Suddenly the mist veers to the side and I look up to find myself once again standing outside the library doors.

"Oh, typical," I mutter with a little shake of my head. I had meant a far more figurative need, but apparently the academy mistook my request. It isn't going to provide me the answer of my problems, all it will do is remind me that I spent the day moping in an observatory and neither the patterns of the stars nor the birds flying past the academy are going to help me graduate this academy as Menavillion's knight champion.

I sigh and push open the door because the academy isn't actually wrong. I do need to study. Maybe I'll grab a book on the history of high fae families and bring it back to my room to read. Assuming that Chastmir doesn't oppose to me using my magic to dimly illuminate the room. I wonder how deep of a sleeper she is.

Marvin always slept through my late-night wanderings and habits. Indeed, I usually stayed up late at night because it was the only time my magic was even useful. Nobody needs a glowing orb in broad daylight.

I frown as I step through the library because the mist doesn't immediately disappear like it did when it led me here earlier or when it brought me to the banquet hall. Instead, it continues onward and disappears behind a shelf.

"Odd," I mutter to myself as I step after it. Perhaps there is a particular book it wants me to read. Maybe one on finding your purpose when you feel bad because your rival wants the same thing that you do, and he was actually a sort of nice guy before he became your rival. I'm not sure if I'll find something half as specific as that, but I don't know all the books this library carries. Most of them are probably on tactics and fae etiquette and histories because those are the things that a knight champion will need the most, but that doesn't necessarily mean that those are the only books here.

After all, this one room contains more books than all of Woodsbury. I think I've read all the books our small town has to offer three times over. It will take me some time to do the same here, and I probably won't have time to do so between my attempts to best Byron and gain Menavillion's favor, but I do hope to be able to discover some new adventures.

I always liked the books with knight heroes best, but maybe that was because of my ambitions.

I round the bookshelf and draw to a sudden halt. "Oh," I gasp out. The sound penetrating the still air. My hand flies to my mouth to stifle myself, but I'm too late and Byron sits up stirring from where he had been laying slumped over a round table toward the back of the library. A piece of paper is sticking to his cheek as he blinks around blearily.

My eyes dart down to the white mist then back up to Byron, then down to the mist then back up to Byron. I'm hoping for the mist to suddenly change directions and lead off into a section of the library, but it remains exactly where it is. Leading straight up to the table and disappearing near Byron's boots.

I swallow hard. "It's you."

"*Lo?*" Byron asks his voice husky. He reaches up to rub at his face, dislodging the paper, but his face is riddled with red imprints from the wood of the table. He exhales loudly as he glances down at the table and then back at me. "I must have fallen asleep...what hour is it?"

"Late," I reply softly. My mind is refusing to process anything.

I'd asked to be led toward what I truly wanted. And it brought me to *Byron*?

Oh, Maker, this academy is trying to play games with my head. Except the academy isn't actually sentient, and the mist is a mere enchantment. What reason would either of them have to fool me?

Much like a fae that has been trapped by his words, things that don't live cannot lie.

Byron presses his hands over the open book that he had been reading before shaking his head and turning back to me, he stifles a yawn. "What are you doing here?"

I open my mouth to reply but perhaps guilt has eaten at me enough or maybe it's that dratted mist on the ground confusing me because I don't want to talk to him angrily or argue. "I didn't mean to wake you. I didn't think that you would be in here."

I step closer, testing the mist to see if it will change at all if I come closer to him. All it does is disappear where my boot touches it, but it remains doggedly pointing to Byron. I perch on the end of the table next to the stacks of books he had piled up. "What were you reading?" I ask, fingering the rough edges of the pages. Byron has to lean back to look at me, which is a nice change for once. Now that there is only a foot of space between me and it, I can determine that it was not leading to any of the books on Byron's desk.

No, it was leading to the blacksmith's grandson himself.

Byron purses his lips. "You know, Willow, I always admired you."

I stiffen slightly at his words.

He tilts his head. "You were always ambitious and resourceful, and you never let anyone talk down to you. I think eventually if we had stayed home, you would have caught my eye. I would have realized what a brave beautiful young woman you were."

I arch my brow. "If you're trying to seduce me so I'll give up on my aspirations toward Menavillion's patronage, I'm going to stop you right there. It will take more than a pretty face to keep me from my dreams."

Byron slides his hand over mine, trapping it against the hard wood. "You think my face is pretty?"

I snort. "Doesn't everyone? Well, at least when it isn't covered in red marks it is."

He tilts his head a small hesitant smile playing on the corner of his lips. "I'm getting off topic. The fact of the matter is that I'm a bit smitten with you." His hand begins to slide up my arm, gliding over my shoulder and coming to a stop just at the nape of my neck. "And I think that would have happened even if we stayed home and we weren't thrust on an adventure together."

He pushes out of his chair so that now he is leaning over me, one hand braced on the table beside me and the other still braced against my neck. The space between our noses seems to be disappearing. "One day, I would have been walking home, and I would have spotted you on that moss covered path yelling at one of the younger boys for teasing poor little Annifred for her lisp, and I would have fallen hard for your spirit and passion just like I did yesterday. And I would have wondered why I was such a fool to never notice you all those years growing up in the same small village."

My head is spinning. I can barely breathe, and I certainly can't think, but I seem to be capable of realizing that the white mist has disappeared.

"I would have screwed up my courage to talk to you." His breath washes over my lips sending the world spinning. The only secure thing here is Byron's arms around me. "It would have been late autumn and in the middle of the harvest festival. I would have taken your hand." His hand slides across the table until it finds mine and he gives it a squeeze. "And I would've led you off alone. There's a still pool in the woods where weeping willows grow, it's magical there at night. And there as the dragonflies dart around us, illuminated by the harvest moon, the stars, and the dim light of fireflies I would have told you how I'd come to feel."

His eyes drop to my lips. My heart is thundering in my chest and my breath coming out in broken huffs. He is going to kiss me, and in this moment, I want nothing more than to let him do so. A hundred alarms ring in my head, but my thoughts are too clouded to hear any of them.

"And then I would have kissed you." His eyes drift shut, and he leans forward, but he stops, his lips a hairsbreadth from my mouth. I have only to lift up my chin to close the gap. But I'm frozen as if he has spoken some sort of stone spell over me. Frozen as he jerks away, leaving me suddenly chilled by the lack of his presence. His eyes have that angry glint in them again as he looks at me, there's something else in them that is just a little fractured. "Except that never would have happened. Because you hate me."

He turns to leave, but suddenly I'm free from my stone spell. My hand darts out and grasps his sleeve. "Byron," I whisper, my voice ragged.

He turns back to me, and I reach up, firmly grasping him by the sides of his head and pull his head back toward mine. My lips greedily find his, demanding the kiss they were nearly denied.

My fingertips skim the pulse on his neck as my lips move across the length of his mouth, from the quirk where they always turn up in that dragon's blasted smirk down to his full bottom lip which I catch between my teeth.

Byron lets out a low growl as he pushes against me, kissing fervently. It almost feels as if my heart will burst. It is beating so quickly and the next thing, I'm processing my back is hitting the table. Byron is on top of me, his arms braced on either side of my head, essentially trapping me.

But I don't feel trapped.

I want more. More of this, more him. This kiss has consumed me and left me nothing but a greedy husk that only wants *him*.

And that is the thought that scares me.

White panic shoots through me, and I shove at him. Byron lifts up just enough for me to somehow slide out from under him although I have no idea how I managed to extricate myself. I stand next to the table my chest heaving as I look at Byron who is now braced on the table looking at me with equal passion and... *fear*.

"Willow," he begins.

I whirl on my heel.

"Willow, wait!"

I don't wait though; I race through the door and I don't look back until I'm safe in the dark confines of my shared room.

CHAPTER SIXTEEN

My mind is a mess right now, but that's nothing compared to how my emotions feel. I need to get my act together, I know this. I didn't work this hard, hold on to my dream for so long just to let one little kiss get into my head and drive me to fail my studies.

I have done a rather admirable job at avoiding Byron, however. So, I'm not totally incompetent.

Now I'm stressing in a private alcove off the training room, trying to calm my nerves so that I can concentrate on this upcoming mock battle. I feel completely unprepared, but just because I haven't been able to focus as much as I should this past week at the academy doesn't mean that I didn't have some practice from my time in Woodsbury. I used to turn the woods beyond Marvin's father's farm into an obstacle course that I had to make it through in record time.

I'm strong, I'm fit, and as untrained as I am as long as I keep my focus, I should be able to hold my own.

Focus is the problem though, isn't it?

I take a bite out of my apple that I brought along because I was too nervous to eat breakfast and yet I also know that I need to keep my strength up.

Marvin sighs loudly, looking up from where he is fastening on leather gauntlets to protect his arms. "Willow, I can't help but get the feeling that something is bothering you."

"I'm *fine*."

"And this has nothing to do with the fact that Byron is moping as well?" he presses.

I pause mid-stretch, the apple held in place by my teeth. I reach up to dislodge it. "Byron has been moping?"

"He'd probably prefer it if I used the term "*brooding*", but yeah, he's been a bit of a mess of late. Just like you." Marvin regards me with narrow eyes. "Did something happen between you two?"

I'm tempted to just shrug off his concern since I still don't want to talk about it. But then I realize that he could ask Byron, and I would rather he hear it from me.

I puff out a breath as I begin making certain that my training leathers are on properly for the mock battle. "I finally told Byron how I feel about him."

Marvin's eyebrows shoot up. "Well, I have no idea why he wouldn't handle that well. You've only hated him since you were a kid."

I nibble on my lip as I shake my head. "And then I kissed him."

"You *what*?" Marvin gasps out, he begins choking on air.

"I kissed Byron," I mumble under my breath as I duck my head. "And he kissed me back, I'll have you know." My heart rate picks up a bit thinking of how he kissed me back.

"What would possess you to *kiss* him, Willow?"

"I don't know," I reply, smacking my thigh with my free hand. The other I flex my fingers around my apple although I still haven't much of an appetite for it.

"I do know," Marvin replies pursing his lips, "But I don't think you're ready to hear it from me."

"Oh, don't give me that, Marvin," I say moving over and sitting down next to him. I nudge him with my shoulder. "You're my friend, it's your duty to tell me when I'm confused. Indeed, you seem to know my emotions better than me sometimes."

He holds up his hands to stave off my buttering up. "It's the same reason that you have always fixated on Byron, I think." He pauses, licking his lips.

"Come on, spit it out already."

"The last thing you have ever felt toward him is apathetic."

"Yeah, because I despise him. Always have."

"No, you're jealous of him and you're jealous *for* him."

"What?" I demand with a scoff. "You're talking nonsense now, my friend."

"You despise Byron not because of anything he does or is, but because you want what he has."

I squirm a little bit. His words, though harsh, perhaps carry a little credence. I *have* always been jealous of Byron's grandfather and magic and standing in town.

"And because you want *him*."

I whip my head, narrowing my eyes. "Didn't your father teach you not to lie?" I demand with a scoff.

"I've seen how uncontrollably angry you become whenever Byron looks twice at another girl. It's as plain as day to me, you just don't want to admit that you don't actually hate him. That the intense feeling you have welling up inside of you when it comes to that boy is love."

I lean away from him, but Marvin presses a hand over mine. "I don't blame you, Willow. You've always been a loner. You like other people, and they like you, but have you ever truly experienced real unconditional *love*? Because that's certainly not something that your parents ever taught you, or any single member of Woodsbury. Sure, they took care of you, but no single soul took you in. My father should have adopted you, I wanted him too. Maybe, then you would have understood that side of your feelings."

I shove my apple into his hand since I know that he will at least make sure it doesn't go to waste and push to my feet, moving away from him. "You're speaking nonsense. You're lucky you're not a fae or else I would demand that you never lie again as recompense for this untruth."

He shakes his head with a small chuckle. "Oh, Willow, stubborn till the last."

I stride past him and do a backwards handstand. "You should be more focused on the upcoming mock battle than my affairs," I grumble, sending him an upside-down glare.

"Oh, I'm not worried. I know I won't win, and I intend to surrender pretty early on to save myself some unnecessary pain. There will always be the next mock battle. But that's not a concept you understand, is it?" Marvin takes a bite from his apple. "Because you will never give in, even if it kills you."

CHAPTER SEVENTEEN

My heart is beating so fast and so loudly in my ears that it nearly drowns out all other sounds around me. I take a deep breath, vainly attempting to calm my nerves as I step into the wide circular chamber where the mock battles are to be held, and immediately regret every choice I've ever made.

Because standing right there, entering the chamber from the other end of the hall is Byron. At the sight of him, all reasonable thought flees my mind, replaced only by panic. Blind and sheer panic that it takes me seeing Chastmir to remember that for this battle the women and men are separated and will only be fighting their own gender.

Byron will just be fighting his opponent at the same time as me, not us two having to go up against each other, but still the timing couldn't be more disastrous. How am I supposed to focus on my own fight with him right there?

I give myself a little shake as I look up into the booths built into the walls where the fae lords and teachers here at the academy are watching from. It takes a short scan for me to find the one that Menavillion is sitting in. He has Istaria at his right and standing behind them both is that silent golden knight who I hope someday to work closely with.

I flick my eyes down, determining to focus solely on that and not what is happening on the other platform. I climb onto one across from Chastmir, I wonder if I'm supposed to bow or do something else to acknowledge the rivalry, but she just lowers herself, bracing her legs into a fighting stance. I give my roommate a once over, taking in her honed muscular arms and tightly coiled golden hair and determine that this girl knows her fighting. She's probably been practicing while I've been spending my time fretting. I exhale a small breath and bend my knees, bracing my legs and get ready to fight for my life. However, just then the platform shifts under my feet. I glance down to see that it has broken away from the rest of the floor. I glance up at Chastmir, but she doesn't seem phased in the least as we lift into the sky. A quick peek to my right shows that the platform the boys are on is also rising. They both stop when they reach halfway up the room.

I'm so stunned that I nearly miss the gong that sounds signifying that the mock battle has begun. Chastmir lets out a cry which is more than a little intimidating as she races toward me. My eyes widen, and I duck from under her sweeping arms. Up this close, I realize that Chastmir is *much* taller than I had expected. Given her golden hair and muscular physic I would venture that she is from the northern islands across the sea from Commonweald. People from those islands are renown for their fierceness in battle.

Which is all stuff that I should have planned for.

I *would* have planned for if only my head had been clearer. I duck again, doing a flip and swinging my legs up nailing a kick on Chastmir. It staggers her but not nearly as much as I would have liked. I chance a glance over my shoulder to see if Menavillion noticed how nimble I was, but stall when I see that he is leaning over talking to Istaria, not paying the least amount of attention to the mock battle. Indeed, the only one in his box who seems to care the least about what is going on is the golden knight, and he is looking toward Byron's platform.

I see a flash out of the corner of my eye and whip my head around, as I realize that I allowed my focus to slip for too long. I try to dodge, but it's too late. Chastmir pounces on me, her hand wrapping around the front of my shirt. I feel my eyes widen as with a roar she deadlifts me. My feet grapple for the ground as she turns and heaves me to the side. I go flying through the air. My hand reaches out, but I can't get a purchase on the platform and only wind up scraping up my forearm before I go flying off.

I gasp out as open air welcomes me and then I go plummeting over the distance at the end of the platform. I have only a second as I fall through the air to reconsider all the life decisions that got me to this point before I land hard on the ground, a crack going through my back. I struggle to inhale, but no breath enters my lungs as I lie there gasping like a fish that has been removed from the water.

Overhead, I see Byron poke his head over the side of the platform where his own fight is taking place. His eyes dart across the floor until they lock on mine, scanning me over as if to assess if I'm all right, but just then a fist flies into his face while his head is turned, and he goes plummeting off his own platform.

I gasp, feeling the wind shift as Byron lands with a crash near me. I get up, with some struggle and drag myself toward him, grimacing as all the bones and muscles in my body protest the movement.

He's already on his elbow, reaching toward me. "Are you all right?" he croaks out. I grimace but manage a nod.

"I was about to ask you the same thing," my voice is airy, and I think that talking might have been a bad idea because I can't draw enough air into my lungs to refill them.

I lay my head down as a voice booms out. "And we have this round's winners, Chastmir and Wilson!"

"I think I'll just lay here for a second," I murmur, disappointment welling up in my heart. I failed my first mock battle, and the fact that Byron did so too is no consolation. It should be, but I can't force myself to celebrate that small victory. Not when the first feeling that surged through me when he fell from that platform was an overwhelming concern for his well-being.

Byron nods as he lays his head down, his eyes locked on mine. "Yeah, me too."

CHAPTER EIGHTEEN

"That looks like it hurts."

I pause in getting dressed and turn to see Chastmir standing near her bed. She nods to the bandage wrapped around my forearm. I grimace as the sheer material of my gown slides over it, not doing much to hide the clunky white material that clashes with it terribly. "I wish I could say that the thing that truly hurts is my pride, but that would be a lie. They both hurt."

She steps toward me, a rueful smile on her face. "I am sorry, I didn't want to hurt you. May I?"

I nod and turn the back of my dress to her as she begins doing up the pearl buttons on the back. It's one of the dresses that Istaria gave me and probably the finest thing to grace my skin. Perfect for a dinner with a fae lord.

"Which fae lord are you hoping to garner the patronage of?" she asks as she steps back.

"Menavillion. You?"

"Whoever will have me." She replies with a shrug.

"Are you coming to the dinner tonight then?" she hesitates a second before shaking her head, her face falling a little.

"What's the matter?"

She lifts a single shoulder. "I don't know, I'm fine with fighting for them, but the thought of sharing dinner with a fae terrifies me. You know to my people the fae are known as the Fair Folk. You don't walk with the Fair Folk, Chastmir. That's what my pa used to always say."

"So why are you trying to become a fae's champion?"

"For a favor, why else? A sickness has ravaged my people for as long as I can remember. It stole my mother from me and turned my father into a cruel man. I will ask for the cure of this disease in return for my servitude to the fae."

"Oh," I say after a brief silence. "That's very honorable."

"What do you wish to gain from Menavillion?" she inquires, tilting her head so that her braid falls to the side.

I nibble the edge of my lip. "It's not going to sound nearly as worthy a cause as yours."

"It's something you are willing to swear away your future for so clearly it's important to you."

I ball my hand into a fist. "I'd like to ask for more magic, so that I can no longer be considered less-than the rest of my kind."

"I cannot fault you for that," Chastmir replies stepping back. She offers me a tight smile. "I wish you the best in your endeavors. If I can, I shall attempt to gain the interest of a different fae so that you can have yours."

"Thank you," I reply with a small smile in return. Perhaps this year won't be so bad after all. So, what if I failed my first mock battle? I will have plenty other opportunities to prove myself in the future. My time at this academy is only just beginning.

"Besides, I've heard rumors that Menavillion would like to leave the academy within the week so that he can return to his affairs. I assume that word of his early departure means he at least has an idea of who he will be taking with him. I hope it's you."

My stomach drops at her words as I realize that I don't have time to improve. I need to be better now, and I have this banquet to prove to him that I'm the person he should be bringing home not Byron.

The question is just *how*?

"Would it truly be the end of the world if Menavillion didn't choose you as his knight?" Marvin asks fidgeting with the ends of his decorated tunic. I think that he is just as uncomfortable all dressed up like this as I am.

"Yes," I reply stonily, mad that Marvin would even speak of a scenario where that would happen even if it's all I've been able to think about since leaving my room.

Marvin shakes his head. "You could always try to get your magic from a different fae lord, I know that not every fae will trade in magic, but there have to be some others here who will. And Byron has a real reason for needing Menavillion's patronage."

I whip my head around. "Wait you've taken his side now?" I demand but before Marvin can respond I whirl on him, clutching my skirts so I don't trip. "What has he told you?"

Marvin opens his mouth but then closes it. He swallows hard, his eyes so wide that he puts me in mind of an owl. "It...it isn't my story to share. All I'm saying is that perhaps you should speak with him. This silent treatment and rivalry thing is really quite juvenile, and I think it's gotten to Byron's head. He's barely sleeping anymore."

I bite down on my lip. I want to argue with Marvin, tell him that it's taking its toll on me to the point where I can barely focus, but I refrain from it for fear of him stating that it's all my fault, and I created a problem out of nothing. That I made this rift between me and Byron that's clearly affecting us both. Or worse he will once again falsely claim that the only reason that I've detested Byron since we were children was because I actually liked him and just didn't know how to process those emotions.

Maybe he would be right, but it's not something I want to hear right now. Much like when I was a child, I'm having a hard time processing anything right now. All I know is that I have a banquet to attend, a fae lord to impress, and I must do it all while not tripping over the long skirts of my dress.

I suppose it's a good thing that Istaria gave me clothes as her repayment to me because I've never seen anything half as fine as this dress, let alone owned it. I'd be showing up in my torn tunic and leggings instead of looking like an otherworldly princess of the sky. The gauzy skirts are multiple layered and see through revealing the skirts underneath each taking a darker and darker hue. The fitted bodice has beads hanging from it that look like stars twinkling against the blue skirts.

If I wasn't so worried about tripping and falling on my face then this dress would give me some much needed confidence, but instead it delivers it with a good level of self-consciousness. The dress is gorgeous, it's me that's the problem. I don't know how to properly wear it.

When I'm a knight, at least I'll be able to wear armor and no longer have to worry about gowns and banquets and impressing people. I'll only have to worry about Menavillion's safety and honor and valor and other things that I feel much more suited for than dressing like a noble lady.

My nerves are feeling rather unsteady by the time we reach the large doors of the banquet hall. "I don't know if I can do this," I whisper to Marvin, my foot stalling a bit.

Marvin continues walking, throwing a quick, "If you don't go, then Byron wins."

That isn't half as motivating as it should be. Which causes me to pause and wonder if Byron winning would be the worst thing that could happen to me. I'd be forced to set my sights on a different fae patron but I'm sure that I could figure something out. And then Byron would go with Menavillion and... well, that's the part that causes me some pause. Byron would be gone; he would no longer be living just down the street in the blacksmith's hut.

No, he would be off serving a high lord in a castle in Skyshire far away and I'll likely be at my own patron's palace in the sky. No matter how this banquet goes we're destined to go our own separate ways. And for some reason at this moment that thought worries me more than the one that Byron might serve Menavillion instead of me.

"Marvin!" I hear Byron call as my friend steps into the banquet hall. "Glad you made it, but you might want to be careful, or Willow will think that you have designs on Menavillion and decide that you're her enemy as well."

I draw in a shaky breath as I step into the room behind Marvin and plastering on a smile. "No, I already know that Marvin is only attending today because he wants to have another look at the fae who has stolen his fancy. And it's *rival,* Byron Coalbiter, not enemy."

I pause again because as soon as I stepped out from behind Marvin. The smirk falls off Byron's face and is replaced by a look that I can't quite interpret. It's a tentative mixture of surprise and fear. He swallows so hard that I can see his Adam's apple bob.

"What?" I demand, glancing down at myself wondering if I have something staining my skirts.

He blinks once, that's the only half a second I have where his eyes are not trained on me. He is frozen in place a little like a deer caught in the hunter's sights who is too afraid to move and draw even more attention to it. "Nothing. It's just... I don't think I've ever seen you in a dress before."

I glance down at myself, rubbing at my skirts. I look back up at him wrinkling my nose. The shoulders that I always thought made me fit to be a knight looking clunky and too broad in this dainty and beautiful gown. "Does my lack of experience in dressing up show? Marvin told me I look fine, but I feel like a rainbow duck all preened like this."

Byron is still staring at me before he blinks once and clears his throat, the floor finally drawing his attention away from me. "No, that isn't it at all. You look beautiful, Lo..." he grimaces. "Willow, I mean."

I nod my head, feeling my stomach twist a little bit. He said it so begrudgingly... The Byron I knew back in Woodsbury would never have hesitated to compliment a person, least of all a beautiful woman.

So, either he doesn't actually see me as beautiful and is simply saying this to be nice, or he doesn't actually want to be nice to the likes of me and he hates that he has to compliment me.

I don't know which I'd rather have be true, both seem like pretty bleak outcomes to me.

I move past Byron into the banquet hall. Two of the tables have been removed and now only one single table remains down the center of the room. It is laden with trays of food and flickering candles which provide some much needed light to the room.

Now that the room is not full of clambering, hungry academy students I realize that one wall is entirely made up of windows with a glass door in the center that leads out into what appears to be a balcony. Through them I can make out the beautiful pink hues of the setting sun, some stars are already visible in the blue above the pink where night is descending slowly.

The room is not nearly as crowded as I had feared, perhaps other potential knights were deterred by rumors of Menavillion's upcoming departure. They likely figured that they would have better chances with a different fae lord who will actually take the time to remain at the academy longer to watch their growth and better make his choice. There are three or four other knights here, I don't recognize their faces, but then I haven't exactly socialized. I guess, I'm a little more like my roommate Chastmir than I'd thought, I'm just less open and honest about it. I'm not here to make friends or get distracted. I'm here to become a knight and that's it.

And yet I've allowed Byron to drive me to utter distraction. How frustrating.

Istaria is standing off to the side having a low, heated conversation with the golden knight. Menavillion appears to be reading a letter at the end of the table, and the dining hasn't started yet so I take this as an opportunity to finally go up and speak with him.

However, I slow a step as I pass Istaria when I realize just how agitated she looks. The glitter sparkling around her eyes catches in the light as she gives her head a sharp jerk. "This is exactly the answer we have been looking for to free you from your service without anyone having to get hurt. I have risked *everything,* and you cannot even risk *him*?" she hisses. "Do you even care about—" at just that moment she looks up, her eyes narrowing as she sees me. "What do you want, wild fae?"

"Well, actually my name is Willow... and as far as I know, I'm not actually a wild fae," I say nervously, wondering what I just walked up on. Clearly, it wasn't something that Istaria wanted me to overhear, then she also usually acts this cold towards me. I swallow as I glance between Istaria and the golden knight then back to Istaria my smile slipping away when I take in her hair whipping through the air like angry snakes, despite the fact that they have been bound up in braids. "You're still cursed."

"You're just as observant as ever," she says with a sniff. "Yes, my *beloved*," she says this with a pointed look at the golden knight, "fiancé is eager to bring me back to his court because nothing he has tried here has managed to free me from this curse."

"Oh," I say, eyeing her hair wondering how long it took her to get it braided with that harsh wind surrounding her whipping it every which way. I can imagine that it would get to be quite annoying after a while, even if it doesn't appear to actually hurt her. I wonder why the cultists would put such a harmless curse on her, but then I suppose there is much about the occult that I do not understand.

The knight steps forward. "I'm actually happy you came over here, I've been meaning to speak with you."

"You have?" I squeak, pointing to myself. Does he remember that night we arrived at the academy and were named as Istaria's saviors? How else would he know me out of the group?

"Don't you dare talk to her," Istaria hisses. The knight ignores me and reaches up, pulling his helmet off. For a second, I think Byron has figured out some way to play a prank on me, but when I look over my shoulder I see that Byron is still behind me. Speaking to Marvin. I turn back around to find myself looking into a very familiar and yet slightly off face. This man... he's identical to Byron. Only his hair is black instead of dark brown and a little shorter than Byron's, but his eyes, his face... his *smirk*.

My mouth drops open, and he lets out a chuckle. "My name is Calder Coalbiter. As I'm sure you've already noticed, I'm Byron's twin."

"*Twin?*" is all I'm capable of gasping out.

"Indeed, and I was hoping that you would talk my brother out of his foolish notion of taking my place as Menavillion's servant since I apparently cannot."

"She certainly will not!" Istaria snaps loudly.

"Calder!" Byron says as he hurries across the room. "What are you doing?"

"*Twin*?" I say again like some sort of mimiceer bird.

Byron turns to me as he reaches me. His eyes pleading and look far more vulnerable than I've seen him since I said those horrible things to him in the library. "Please, ignore whatever it is my brother is trying to tell you."

"You have a brother?" I demand, my voice coming out rushed and breathy.

"Who is ready to eat?" Menavillion calls as he sets aside the letter that he had been reading. The other knights begin moving to seats at the table, but Marvin is standing in the middle of the room staring at us with confusion, obviously wondering what it is that this small huddle is discussing. I wish I knew, but I'm quite at a loss despite being in the middle of everything being discussed.

Byron grasps my arm and begins to pull me away. "I can explain..."

"Explain what?" Calder demands, "The fact that you are willing to give up your whole life for a brother that you've never met until just recently and apparently never cared about enough to speak of to your friends?"

"That isn't fair," Byron growls. "And how dare you try to use Willow against me." He gestures to me. "Why would you even think that I'd listen to her?"

"Because I saw how you looked at her. If you won't listen to me then fine, I will turn everyone you care about against this idea," Calder growls out. His eyes are cold and I decide that he doesn't look very much like Byron at all. "You will not be taking my place."

"The bargains I strike will be between me and Menavillion," Byron replies, his voice as firm as steel. "You will not have a say in the matter."

"As well he shouldn't," Istaria says shrilly. "Calder, leave well enough alone. If your brother is willing to give up his freedom for you, then I say let him."

"No," Calder says.

"Yes," Byron says.

"What is going on?!" I yell.

Silence answers me, and that's when I realize that everyone else had been speaking in low tones. Now, all eyes turn to me at my loud outburst. Including Menavillion's...

CHAPTER NINETEEN

Confusion and mortification are the two emotions warring within me. Both are telling me to get out of here, find some space, and clear my head.

I draw in a sharp breath and turn on my heel, ducking around Byron who is trying to say something to me. I make a beeline to the balcony, it's probably not as far as I would like to run, but right now it is my best option.

The cool air brushes against my skin through the sheer material of my sleeves as I step outside. The glass doors crash shut behind me. I feel embarrassed, I know I can't be making the impression I want to Menavillion, and yet I can't help but feel like I've been kicked in the stomach. I lean forward on the banister my mind whirring. Byron... has a twin brother?

How can someone I've known my whole life surprise me this much?

There is a slight creak behind me and suddenly the balcony gets a whole lot warmer as someone joins me out here. A loud sigh sounds behind me. "Willow, I can explain."

"Explain how you managed to hide a whole entire person from me, Byron," I demand whirling.

He winces as he reaches up to rub the back of his neck. "Calder is... not a subject we broach much in my home. It's still too sensitive, and we didn't want the whole town knowing. We'd already lost enough without being a spectacle as well."

"What do you mean? What are you talking about?" I ask, stepping toward him. I glance toward the glass windows, but they are simply reflected with the sunset. It paints a false sense of security, making me think that maybe we're alone, but the truth is that everyone on the other side of that window may very well be watching us.

Byron bites down on his lip as he glances down, scuffing at the tiles on the floor of the balcony with his foot. "Calder is how my family got their magic."

I shake my head slightly. "I'm not following."

"When my mother was a young woman, she sought to live a life above what was afforded to a blacksmith's daughter, so she went to Skyshire. And that's where she met Menavillion." Byron purses his lips as he moves to the railing, I turn following him with my eyes as he braces himself against it. "They struck a bargain. He would give her magic to rise above her station and in return for that she would give him her.... She would give him her..."

He pauses, grimacing as if the words pain him.

"She gave him her firstborn," I whisper softly. Such a thing is not entirely uncommon, fae have been known to bargain for all sorts of unnatural things. It's part of the reason why I wanted to become a knight. I would give myself in noble and honorable service in exchange for magic instead of anything a fae might suggest.

"Indeed. It nearly destroyed my family when he came to collect my mother's firstborn when she had us. He took Calder, and father blamed her. He left the day after. Mother turned to drinking, and it was just grandfather and myself after that, but I suppose even with grandfather I had more family than Calder ever did. He was raised by a fae far away in Skyshire."

I whip my head to Byron, my thoughts that have been clouded all week finally clearing. Pieces fall together as Istaria's and Calder's conversation begins to make more sense. "That's why you want to serve Menavillion," I gasp out. "You're going to swear your service to him in return for him giving your brother his freedom."

Byron nods slowly. "I should have told you sooner, I guess I just didn't want you pitying me. I'd rather you hate me than pity me, Willow."

I reach out, resting a hand on his arm. "I never hated you. I..." I trail off as a new thought catches up with the dozens swirling around in my head. "But Byron, you would be selling your freedom in exchange for his."

"Calder doesn't want me to do it," he replies, pulling his arm away. "But he doesn't realize that Woodsbury would be better off with him in it than me. Mother always said that she wished I'd been born first that way she could have Calder. And my brother deserves the chance to get to know Grandfather before he passes on..."

"You cannot honestly believe that," I say, my voice suddenly coming out stern. "Byron Coalbiter, no one will be better off without you."

He looks over at me, surprised the wind picking up bits of his hair and blowing the stands across his cheekbones. I raise my hands, hesitating a second before I rest them on either side of his face, forcing him to look me in the eye. "Least of all me."

His eyes brighten for a second but then dim with sadness. "I have to do this. It's what I've worked my whole life toward. I've found a way to secure my brother's freedom and a way out of my mother's hastily made bargain. What sort of person would I be if I let my family down?" He lifts a single shoulder. "It won't be all bad. I think I'd enjoy being a knight, besides you can't honestly tell me that this is a bad fate when it's what you're striving toward as well."

"I'm doing this of my own free volition," I say. "You're forcing yourself into a decision that should not be taken lightly."

He reaches up, grasping my wrists gently. He pulls them away from his face, pressing a quick kiss to the insides of my wrists before giving me a wry smile that does not reach his eyes. "My mind is made up, but I've been thinking and I'm hoping that perhaps if I can convince Menavillion to take me then he will be giving up one of his guards. He wants two knight champions. I could put in a good word for you. We can both get what we want and be our own little part of Woodsbury all the way out in Skyshire."

"I—Byron, I..."

"Please say *yes*." His eyes hold mine. "I need someone to support me in this. Please, Willow, I'll find a way to get you your position as well and we can finally be allies instead of rivals."

"But—" I begin. Before I can manage to make sense of my swirling thoughts, there is a screech from inside, followed by the sound of breaking glass. Byron and I break apart and share a worried glance, before we both race back into the banquet hall.

CHAPTER TWENTY

Wind tears at my hair, whipping through my skirts, sharp and cold like what would be found at the heart of a tempest. And yet we are inside now.

I hold my hand up, my eyes stinging as my hair whips into it, trying to figure out what is happening. Through the tears building up, I can see Marvin and the other knights hanging on to the table as food and small plates are whipped through the air in a circular motion.

Menavillion is on his knees, his head thrust back and his mouth hanging open. His eyes appear to have rolled back so that only the milky white of it shows, and he is shuddering while still oddly locked into place as if he is held there by some invisible barrier that is so tight that only the slightest of shivers can escape that invisible prison.

Istaria is facing him, her back towards us as she slowly backs up several steps. She is yelling. "I'm not going *any-*

where with you! *Nowhere, you hear!"* She throws back her head and chuckles, looking truly unhinged.

She's about to back right into us when suddenly a hand grasps my arm and yanks me to the side. I look over to see that Byron is being pulled aside as well. Calder has a hold of both of us, his golden armor looking closer to bronze in the darkness, and his hair whipping around his head. We're dragged forward until we're almost to the door when I dig in my heels. "What's going on?" I call, struggling to be heard over the rushing wind.

"I'm doing what I have to in order to protect my family," Calder replies, his tone cold as an ice bath.

Byron rips his hand out of Calder's hold. "What have you done?" he demands.

"Nothing myself," Calder says with a small smile. "But you wouldn't listen to me, you wouldn't accept the fact that I was a lost cause, and you were so stubbornly intent on taking my place like some sort of stupid sacrifice to the slaughter. I couldn't stand idly by while Menavillion made your life a living horror. The man is a cruel and uncaring taskmaster. He had to be destroyed."

"What did you do?" Byron demands, each word ringing out.

"Nothing!" Calder replies again, gleefully. "It was all Istaria. Oh, I played a role in convincing her to fall for me instead of her fiancé, we wrote to each other illicitly during her courtship of Menavillion, but she was bound to him and needed to be free. So, I happened to gift her with a book on dark magic. What she did with that... well, that was on her."

"Dark magic?" I ask with a little shake of my head. "No, that curse was put on her by the..."

"Cultists? Yes, cultists hired by her to use the spell. She feigned a kidnapping so that she would be above suspicion when Menavillion eventually died, but she was doomed from the start. You see, Istaria didn't understand dark magic very well, and she has no idea that this particular spell is too powerful now that it has locked on to Menavillion's magic. As it drains him, it will become only more violent until it knocks this whole wretched academy out of the sky. Then there will no longer be a place for people to compete like horses in a race to catch the eye of any single fae lord."

"Knock the..." I begin, my mind spinning. We're too high up. If anyone falls from this height, they'll die. "You're mad! There are innocent people here."

"Death is a better fate than a life in bondage." Calder jerks his head toward the door. "Now come quickly, I have a dragon waiting. All three of us can escape to safety before

Istaria's spell destroys the academy. We can go back to Woodsbury and no one has to trade away their freedom."

Byron is shaking his head, looking stunned, his mouth opening and closing as if he doesn't know what to say. Honestly, I don't know what to say either, but I doubt words will be enough to save this academy. I whirl as Byron starts yelling at Calder and look over the room. Marvin is being pelted by bits of ham. I glance past him to Menavillion who is trapped in the thralls of the curse.

Then my eyes turn to Istaria who is standing with her back to the balcony. Two thoughts strike me. Istaria's curse can't destroy the academy if she isn't in it, nor would it have much of an affect if she is not near Menavillion who seems to be fueling her powers.

My feet are moving before I realize what is going on as I race forward, fighting against the gusts of wind, dragging myself forward by grasping stones between their mortar and gripping the panes of the windows before I finally reach Istaria. It feels as if a great force is trying to shove me back, but I wrap my arm around her and begin dragging her with me to the end of the balcony.

"What are you doing?" she screeches. "Unhand me!"

I grit my teeth as I tighten my hold. I send up a brief prayer to the Maker, hoping that despite his abandonment he will still accept my soul before I flip us both over the railing.

Behind me I hear Byron scream, "*Willow, n*o!"

But it's far too late and I'm already plummeting through the open air, Istaria is clutched in my arms. And the thought that I had not allowed myself to process finally shines through. *I'm going to die...*

CHAPTER TWENTY-ONE

I'd expected frantic thoughts to fill my mind as I plummet to my inevitable demise. Instead, I'm flooded with pleasant memories—of Byron's smile and Marvin's laugh and the stories Byron's grandfather used to tell me. The way the sun felt on my shoulders, the smell of moist dirt, the sound of the wind moving through the leaves.

I relive all the little things that I hadn't realized that I loved until now, and none of them have anything to do with the academy.

Which would probably surprise me except I'm currently plummeting through the air to what will likely be my death, so I guess it doesn't matter, and I don't actually currently have to unravel what that means.

Suddenly, a whistle sounds overhead I look up just in time to see a figure drop from the balcony, a second later a large-winged shadow takes off, tucking in its wings as it hurtles toward the falling figure who somehow angles itself to land on the creature's back. As soon as both of them are together they swoop toward us and as they do so I get a look at them and realize that it's Byron—no, not Byron... Calder. And he's flying on a yellow dragon.

They plummet towards us, the dragon scooping Istaria and me up in its talons before it extends its wings into a glide. It descends quickly, we are nearing the ground when suddenly a gust of Istaria's wind bursts through the air and crashes into the dragon. It wobbles and bobs, seems to nearly catch itself before losing complete control and falls down.

I go flying out of its claws in the process, hitting the ground hard. Calder lands next to me, but Istaria remains above us, floating several feet above the ground. The wind becomes visible as it cyclones around her due to the amount of dirt it is now pulling up. Chunks of rocks are ripped up and pulled in around her.

Calder pushes himself up on his elbows, and we both watch as Istaria throws back her head and screeches. Then suddenly her whole body goes limp. For a single second, everything hangs suspended in the air and then there is a loud snapping sound, and a shockwave bursts out. The rocks start flying toward us. My eyes widen just as Calder throw himself in front of me, and then the rocks start descending.

I blink my eyes open, confusion wrapped around me like a fuzzy blanket. Where am I? What happened?

My vision starts to clear revealing smooth cut, white stone walls and draping cloths fixed to the ceiling that cascade around the bed that I'm lying in, offering some modicum of privacy. I groan and start to sit up, but just when I try to raise my hand to rub at my face it snags on something. I lift my head, my eyes widening when I see that my hand is trapped between both Byron's hands as he lays slumped against the bed.

His face is turned toward me and I can't help but admire how peaceful he looks right now. There are slight dark circles under his eyes, but all the lines have disappeared. I hesitate a second before reaching my hand and lightly tracing my fingers along the strands of hair that are escaping the tie he has binding his hair at the nape of his neck.

A shuffling sound comes from somewhere deeper in the room.

My eyes flick around, taking in the drapes drifting gently in the soft wind that must be coming from an open window nearby. I gently slide my hand out from between Byron's and slip out of the bed, a shock running up my legs as my bare feet meet cold stone. I'm dressed in a white overlong shirt and matching pants.

I throw one last glance at Byron who is still asleep and step around the gauzy curtain. I draw up short when I see Menavillion standing there. He looks regal again, a distinct contrast to how he looked the last time I saw him when he was locked in those strange convulsions. He is dressed in a red robe that is crimson like blood, and his hair hangs around him in a flawless sheet. I draw up short suddenly feeling self-conscious about my loose clothes and bare feet. I pull the neckline of my shirt more tightly together so that it doesn't gap open and reveal my collar bone. I stand up a little straighter.

"My Lord," I stammer out.

He nods his head in acknowledgement but only spares me the briefest glance toward me, his focus is on something through a gap in some curtains.

"How are you feeling?" I ask moving closer to him so that I can get a glimpse at what he is looking at.

Inside are both Istaria and Calder lying in beds similar to the one that I woke up in. Istaria's hair for once is still, splayed out on the pillow around her. It's my first look at her without the curse and I can see her face clearly. She's truly beautiful. It's hard to believe that she felt the need to get herself cursed, but I suppose that she felt like she was coerced into a marriage then she would have done whatever she felt necessary to keep that fate from happening.

Even cursing herself.

Menavillion exhales loudly, after a long moment. "I believe that question would be more aptly asked you. After all, you're the one who fell from the academy."

I grimace at the reminder and rub at my ribs; through my shirt I can feel a bandage covering the slight cuts the dragon's talons gave me when it caught me.

"I'm alive which is more than I was expecting. What is going to happen to them?" I ask with a nod toward Istaria and Calder.

Menavillion wrinkles his nose in disgust. "If marriage is such a horrible thing that she would go through all that to be rid of me then I will make certain that she can never escape me. I will go through with marrying her, and she will rue the day that she decided to make our arrangement anymore than amicable."

I start slightly and turn to him. "You can do that? You have the power to force her to marry you?"

"She was bound to me the moment her father agreed that she would be my bride. As a fae, she cannot go back on an agreement, therefore she cannot escape which is why she decided to stoop to such unholy means." He shakes his head. "*Cultists*... besides, I'm doing her a favor, if I left her to the justice of the world, she would be dismembered for dealing in dark magic. As the wife of a high fae, she would be above justice."

"And Calder?" I ask with a slight swallow.

"He was a crafty one. I would not have known to suspect him had his brother not revealed his part to me. He never actually dealt with the dark magic, which saves him from dismemberment, but I am his vassal lord. I can punish him as I see fit."

I bite down on my lip as Menavillion finally turns toward me. "But we are straying from the topic at hand. You saved my life, Little One."

I straighten slightly at his words, feeling my eyes round.

"I will be leaving this wretched academy as soon as Istaria and my unfaithful knight are ready to travel, this whole experience has ruined me from trusting anyone. I do not intend to take on another knight anymore, but I owe you a favor so ask whatever you wish of me, and it will be yours."

Menavillion shudders slightly. "And then I can be free to leave this whole affair behind."

I feel my eyes widen as my mouth pops open. Menavillion is leaving? My first thought is to ask him to reconsider not taking on knights and ask me to be his, but then I realize that I can just ask him for magic. I don't need to become a knight. I don't need to prove myself to anyone else. I need only to ask, and I'll finally have everything I ever wanted.

And then I can go back home to Woodsbury and... and what?

My first thought is that I'd finally be worthy of Byron Coalbiter.

And it makes me wonder if I've somehow been doing all this to become worthy of him. Maybe, Marvin was right, and I've always loved Byron but somehow contrived this massive gap between us making it so that he was some unattainable thing. And then I led myself to believe that maybe just maybe if I had magic, I would be good enough for him.

But that could never happen, because Byron's magic isn't what makes him so special.

He's kind and honest, he genuinely cares about people and that's why they like him so much. Not because he is charming or talented, although he is certainly that as well, but because he is a good person.

My eyes flick to Byron's brother who is lying in that bed, so still. Not aware of everything that awaits him. He did nearly kill me, but then he saved me. So, can he be truly entirely evil like I've always been told those who deal in dark magic are?

But more than that. What will Byron do to try to save his brother a second time? From a worse fate than before. He was willing to sell away all his freedoms to become a vassal when he truly didn't want to be...

"A-anything?" I ask.

"As long as it is within reason and lawful to the charter of bargains, then yes."

I exhale slowly, pressing my eyes shut. "I want you to free Calder from his service to you," I spit it out quickly before I change my mind.

Menavillion splutters. "That is not within reason."

"Please," I say stepping toward him. "Don't you believe in second chances?"

He gives his head a sharp shake. "Absolutely not."

"I jumped out a window to save you, My Lord. That wasn't within reason either. All I'm asking for is one man's freedom."

Menavillion purses his lips. "He deserves to be punished."

"He was stolen from his home, and his family when he was just a child, raised to be only your servant and has never known freedom. Ever. I think his life was punishment enough."

Menavillion presses his eyes shut and releases an exhale. "*Very well.*" He holds out his hand and I shake it as his steely gaze locks on me. "I hereby free Calder Coalbiter from my service and all binds that hold him to me. There, now we are even. I wish you a happy life and may we never meet again."

With those words he turns and strides from the room. I turn, looking at the sleeping form of Calder, feeling much lighter than I think I've ever felt.

CHAPTER TWENTY-TWO

I consider following Menavillion out of the infirmary so I can find my rooms and change, but then I realize that if Byron wakes up and I'm gone he would probably wonder and maybe worry. Assuming I'm not overexaggerating my place in his life.

But then... he was asleep next to my bed holding my hand so maybe...?

I shake that thought from my head. I likely ruined any chance of getting together with Byron with the horrible way I acted towards him. It's enough that he will still consider me a friend and I shall just have to manage to find some way to be content with that.

I step back into the room to see that Byron is sitting up, his head whipping around in a panic. He freezes when he sees me and he exhales, his shoulders losing some of their tension.

"Hi," I say nervously as I move over to the bed. I plop onto it, crossing my legs.

"Hi?" he demands. "You fell out of the academy. I thought you were dead. And all you have to say for yourself is *hi*?"

"You sound mad," I say, pulling back slightly.

"I am. I'm relieved too, it's quite the mixture swirling through me right now. What you did there was the craziest most reckless, stupidest thing I have ever seen." He shakes his head and huffs a small breath. "Please don't ever do that to me again."

"I can't promise," I say tilting my head so that all my hair spills over the side. "I'm a crazy, stupid, reckless girl."

"Two of those are true at least." Byron licks his lips as he looks me over. "How are you feeling?"

"Like I fell out of a floating building and got dropped by a dragon, so in other words not the best. But I'll survive."

"You'd better," he replies as he snags my hand; he rubs his thumb over the curve of my knuckle as he shakes his head. "I probably lost a year of my life for every moment I thought you were gone. I'm going to die young now because of you."

"You're not going to die because of an academy you're in falls out of the sky though," I say lightly. "So, I at least bought you a few extra days."

He shakes his head, leaning his head down until he buries it into the mattress. He lets out a loud groan before he raises his head. I notice that he still has my hand firmly clasped in his as he looks me over with those shockingly blue eyes. "What am I going to do with you? Because part of me wants to kiss you passionately and never let you go, and the other wants to wring your neck for what you put me through when I thought you were gone."

"Do I get a vote?" I ask.

His mouth twists wryly.

"Because I vote for the kissing."

"I guess you would with the other option being strangulation."

"No," I say with a swallow. "Not because of that. It's because I.... well, I—" I pause my stuttering and raise my hand to pinch my nose. I want nothing more to tell Byron how I really feel and yet the words are getting all clogged and jumbled in my throat.

"Because, why?" he breathes moving closer, his thumb starts stroking the back of my hand more quickly.

"Where's Marvin?" I ask instead.

"He had to go lay down after everything that happened. I think he lost some years of his life too. Now, what was it you were saying?"

"I spoke with Menavillion. He's leaving without choosing a knight," I say because that's somehow easier to admit to than that I like Byron.

Byron's eyes flick back and forth as if he is looking for some sort of answer as to how he should respond to that. Shock, remorse, and finally frustration wells in his eyes. "I suppose neither of us are getting what we want from him then." He bows his head, finally releasing my hand. "I don't even know what to think of my brother at this point. What he did, it was despicable and yet... he did it because he wanted to protect me. I think he would have continued to be Menavillion's pawn all his life but then I wrote him and told him that I was going to come and take his place. He wrote back, he was always adamant that he didn't want me to make that sacrifice for him and yet I forced his hand. And people nearly died because of it, you nearly died. And oh, Maker... now what will become of him."

"Menavillion offered me a favor in return for saving his life," I state slowly, still unable to believe what I actually did with that favor. And yet I can't find it in myself to regret my actions. I'd do it again if I had to.

The corner of Byron's mouth hitches up. "Did he? Well, it's deserved, don't you think? You did nearly plummet to your death for him."

"I technically did it for the whole academy," I say. "For Marvin and... *you*." The last part comes out in a whisper that is so quiet I'm not sure if he even heard it. I press my eyes shut inwardly groaning. I can't believe this, I never had a problem speaking to Byron when I thought I detested him, but now that I want to admit that he is my sun and my stars, and the words die on my tongue.

"So, what is your new magic like?" Byron asks, leaning back in his chair. He braces his hands on the arms as if waiting for a good display.

"I didn't ask for new magic."

He arches his brow. "You're jesting with me. I know you too well, Willow, you wouldn't give up your opportunity to be as powerful as me."

"I asked Menavillion to free your brother from his service to him," I say, glancing down and picking at a loose string on my bedsheet.

He flinches slightly. "Willow, please, don't do that. This is far too sensitive a subject for you to tease me on it."

"I'm not teasing you." I force my gaze to rise as I look at him.

"But he nearly killed you!"

"I didn't do it for him, I did it for you."

"But you wanted your magic."

"I wanted..." my voice fades out before I can say *you*. I clear my throat. "I wanted to do this for you more."

"But... but..." Byron pushes to his feet, his chair nearly capsizing as he stands. "You hate me."

"I don't *hate* you, Byron Coalbiter. I don't even dislike you. Quite the contrary, actually. I, well... you know how you said if we were back home how you would have handled your feelings for me? Well, if we were back home, I'd have followed you from the harvest festival and let you kiss me by the lake."

Byron's eyes widen slightly but then he exhales and leans closer, bracing himself on the bed. He quirks a brow as he holds my gaze. "And what are you going to do since we aren't home?"

"I suppose I'll just have to settle for kissing you here in this infirmary."

"Willow," Byron says pulling back slightly, looking me over with concern. "Are you sure you're all right? You must have hit your head."

"Please, call me Lo if you want. And I don't think I've ever been quite so certain in my entire life." I push up onto my knees and grasp Byron's shoulders. I guide him down, the bed sags under his weight as he braces a knee next to me. Then I press my lips against his.

EPILOGUE

An ending is only ever a way to experience a new beginning.
—The teachings of Saint Miguel on mortality and the disappearance of the Maker

E arly autumn paints a lovely picture of reds and oranges in the trees around Woodsbury. I hadn't thought that I would be back around this time. I had figured I would still be at the academy, and then after I was picked up by a knight, I would only have precious few days to call my own when my patron decided. I probably wouldn't have had enough time to visit Woodsbury.

I guess I figured that when my days as a knight were up, and I had filled my life with adventure then I would finally settle down back at Woodsbury. But until that time came, I'd travel the world.

Marvin sighs heavily as we approach the bridge that crosses the small stream that winds around the border of Woodsbury. "Do you think Istaria is married by now?"

"I don't think she's gotten married in the last five minutes since you last asked," Byron replies with a roll of his eyes.

Marvin shakes his head. "I just can't believe that Menavillion forced her into marriage. No one should be forced into something like that."

"Marvin, you need to stop pining over her. She nearly got you killed, her selfish actions did get that templar killed," I say, patting his shoulder. "You're *much* better off without her."

"She only did all that horrible stuff because..." Marvin glances at Byron and snaps his mouth shut. "Never mind."

Because of Calder, who did it because of Byron who did it because of his mother who did it because of Menavillion, and it's all just a cycle of blame isn't it? Still, I think whether she thought she was in love or not Istaria should be responsible for her own actions. Calder may have manipulated her, but she still was the one to come up with the horrible idea of hiring cultist and having her guard killed to make it look like a true ambush.

She's Menavillion's problem now, whether he chose to marry her out of revenge or because he truly loved her, I suppose no longer matters. He is far away, and I'll likely never see either of them again.

"Do you think if Istaria had not been so cruelly forced to wed that... she and I—"

"No," Byron says with snort, cutting him off.

I reach out and cuff his shoulder. "Be nice!"

"Of course, darling," he says, his eyes twinkling. He turns back to Marvin. "I'm sorry, but no."

Marvin huffs out a dejected breath but doesn't argue. "I'm going to stay in Woodsbury this time," he mutters. "I don't think I can handle anymore fae. Not you, of course, Willow, but the other ones."

I nod once. "Okay, but you're the one who needs to convince your father to give up on his dreams of you attaining a magical lineage."

Marvin grumbles under his breath and Byron smiles at me as Marvin trudges on ahead. He reaches his hand out, wriggling his fingers. I slide my hand into his and he presses a kiss to it. "You know, you could very well stay here as well. You don't have to go back, Lo."

I'm shaking my head before he finishes his sentence. "I'm not ready to give up on my dream *just* yet, Byron Coalbiter. I still intend to be a knight, perhaps not Menavillion's, but someone else's."

"I'll just miss you so," Byron grumbles.

I stop and rest a hand on his cheek. "I'll miss you too. I'll write you as often as I can."

"You make certain that you do because if a single *day* goes by where I don't hear from you, I'm heading to Skyshire to hunt you down."

I laugh lightly. "I'll have studies."

"I'm more important than those."

"Are you certain that you won't come back to the academy with me?"

He shakes his head. "The only reason I wanted to be a knight is so I could take my brother's place. With him now free, I realize that my place is here, spending time with the man who raised me while he still walks this world." He gives my hand a small squeeze. "Besides, I wouldn't want you to decide that I'm your rival again."

"You'll always be my rival, Byron. Because I'm not going to stop trying to prove to you that I love you better than you love me."

"Oh, that's a challenge I gladly accept," he says with a laugh.

"Please stop," Marvin groans from where he is up the road.

I flash him a grin. "Sorry, Marvin, but I must get all my romantic gushing out of the way before I leave so Byron can have something to remember me by."

"Do you think Gertrude will be heartbroken to hear that Byron is finally claimed?" Marvin asks with a sigh. "I know she had a thing for him."

Byron shrugs. "Maybe that will be an opportunity for you to show your quality. I'm sure she would appreciate a shoulder to cry on."

I smile as I rest my hand on his shoulder as the sound of clanging rings through the air and the smithy comes into view.

"Do you think he will show up?" I ask.

"Calder promised." Just as Byron speaks, I spot a cloaked figure standing in the shadows of the smithy. Byron spots it as well and straightens. "I'm glad you're here to see Calder meet his grandfather. It wouldn't be right to do it without you here."

I turn to Byron, pushing on my tiptoes and plant a quick kiss on his chin. "I'm glad you're glad."

I step back, studying him. I'm trying to store up the memory of this moment, the smell of the autumn wind, the feel of Byron's hand in mine, the blue of his eyes. How it feels to be home.

In Woodsbury with Byron. That's my home.

For a while it will have to be what gets me through as I work toward my dream. But once I'm a knight I'll come back and we'll figure out some way to be together. After all, when two people love each other the way we do what could truly come between us?

Not time.

Not distance.

Not even the end of all things.

Because some things just persevere, and my love for Byron Coalbiter is one of those things.

AFTERWORD

Willow and Byron, as well as Marvin will return in Knight's Fall book one:

To Slay a Knight Boldly

GLOSSARY
THE KNIGHTLY FACTIONS

Gilded Knights

F ounded by one of the five saints, a high fae lord named Edwin Highcastle, these knights choose to serve a powerful lord as their vassal. They attend the Academy of the Gilded Knight and are known as knight champions upon graduation. They are often granted an ability or some other boon in return for their service.

Knights of the Order

Knights who join this faction cherish valor above all else. The saintly founder the Order was a wild fae named Evergreen Hawkheart and those that wish to join this faction attend the Conservatory of the Order and graduate as wardens, dedicated to the protection of mankind and to maintaining communion with nature. All Wardens are Oathsworn, having given their word in some regard in return for a companionship bond with an animal.

Knights of the Brotherhood

This exclusive, secretive, and very rigorous knightly academy was founded by the human saint Lord Constantine Lockwell. Loyalty is cherished above all else by members of this faction. These knights are allowed into the Hall of Brotherhood by invitation only. Graduates are known as templars and what happens within the halls of their order is never spoken of with outsiders.

Hallowed Knights

These selfless knights, dedicate themselves in service of the Maker and of all mankind. Members of this order are celibate in the order drive away any distractions from their holy purpose. Founded by the saintly human monk Ernwood Bitterbloom members of this faction attend the Hallowed Chapel and graduate as paladins. These servant knights are renown healers.

Knights of the Sword

Founded by Pirus Foxshare, the cunning commoner who many believe attained sainthood by his silver tongue alone, this faction has the reputation of being one completely devoid of all honor and goodness. Members attend the Citadel of Swords and graduate as mercenaries who sell their sword arm in exchange for gold. They are commonly known as barbarians by the other knightly factions, however they refer to themselves as sellswords.

Fallen Knights

This order was created in defiance to the Maker's commands, by a dark fae that was no saint. It is the sixth knightly faction, a number that was cursed by the Maker. Those that joined this faction willfully turned their backs on the Maker. They were tainted by dark magic, their order nearly destroyed, and their members scattered, but they are growing in power and not even death can stop a fallen one from completing his role in life....conquest.

Other Classifications...

As well as joining one of these factions, a knight may also choose to earn some boon by swearing a special oath. These knights are known as Oathsworn Knights, not every knight is an Oathsworn, but to become a paladin or warden, one must become one. An Oathbreaker is a knight who has turned their back on their oaths. Such a knight shall be afflicted for this sleight until absolution is found.

Warsworn Knights are berserkers who have been expelled from their order and are a most dangerous lot.

About the Author

Nicki is a twenty-something author of fantasy and YA. She has been writing since she was eleven, and has since published several works. She enjoys creating stories with twisty-stabby faerie romances, retellings that take a darker turn, and epic fantasies in worlds full of monsters and magic.

Nicki lives in Ohio where she spends far too much time watching TV, playing video games, and sleeping. She listens to music basically all the time, and adores obsessing over mythologies, her shows, and her slew of fictional boyfriends. When not writing, she can usually be found at her desk with either a paintbrush or a pen in her hand.

ACKNOWLEDGEMENTS

Publishing this story was a dream come true. I've wanted to publish in a multi author series for some time now, so I leapt at the opportunity to be able to join such an amazing lineup of talented authors.

I just wanted to say a special thank you to Eliza, Jessica, Stephanie, Angela, Alisha, Nicole, Jesikah, Megan, Jes, and Jamie for allowing me to publish my work alongside you. You ladies were such fun to work with. Thank you for endless resources you shared and the hours spent chatting and brainstorming.

To my family for your constant support along the way. Especially my mom for your enthusiasm when I said that I was publishing this.

To my readers for your excitement, as always, when I announced this story.

To my dragons for being the BEST street team ever.

To my editor Eve for the wonderful work that you did.

To my cover designers Mien, Franzi, for everything that you did to bring my ideas to life. And to Maddy for the gorgeous character illustrations of Willow and Byron.

To Jesus for *never* abandoning me.

MORE FAE BY NICKI CHAPELWAY

This trilogy follows Jaye MacCullagh, a human Guardian dedicated to protecting the mortal world from that of the fae of Irish myths. However, when she and her brother find themselves trapped in their home the treacherous Otherworld, and her brother becomes ensnared by an unseelie faerie, Jaye is forced to ally herself to Ravven Crowe. Even if he is a vain and arrogant solitary fae who has plans to make her the Fair Assassin—a human capable of killing the fae.

ALSO BY NICKI CHAPELWAY

An Apprentice of Death (*An Apprentice of Death,* book one)

Harbinger of the End: A Tale of Loki and Sigyn

A Week of Werewolves, Faeries, and Fancy Dresses (*My Time in Amar,* book one)
A Time of Trepidation, Pirates, and Lost Princesses (*My Time in Amar,* book two)
A Season of Subterfuge, Courtiers, and War Councils (*My Time in Amar,* book three)

A Certain Sort of Madness (*Return to Amar,* book one)
A Matter of Curiosity (*Return to Amar,* book two)

A Winter Grim and Lonely (*Winter Cursed*, book 0.5)
Winter Cursed (*Winter Cursed*, book one)
A Winter Dark and Deadly (*Winter Cursed*, book two)

Between Gods and Demigods (*Rage Like the Gods*, book 0.5— available free to newsletter subscribers)
Rage Like the Gods (*Rage Like the Gods*, book 1)

The Gods Created Monsters (*What the Gods Did*, book 1)

A Tale of Gods and Glory: A Standalone Legend

Made in United States
Orlando, FL
21 August 2024

50617680R00143